Angelbots

by
Jack Robertson

You may order Angelbots at Amazon.com (Kindle)

Robertson, John Chester
Angelbots/ John Chester Robertson

First Edition

ISBN 978-1-7322684-4-9

CONTENTS

Abyss 5

Eyes everywhere 9

Fishing 16

Collusion 20

Renso's Robot 26

Directors Revenge 32

Lou's turn 36

Buried Puzzle 40

Others 45

Angelic? 50

Challengers 56

Shenanigans 62

Boomerang 74

Awakening 85

Resolution 98

Mobilization 117

Justice 128

Terry 136

Ghosts 160

Reality 170

Lost 189
Found 205
Dumas 222

Dedications

Courtney T. Dorsey

Connor R. Dorsey

Delanie R. Robertson

Lauren O. Robertson

Angelbots

1

Abyss

Lorenzo is the son of a deceased couple. They raised him in this big house overlooking the river. When his parents estate settled last year, Lorenzo inherited billions. He would give it all back just to be with Angel and Hiker again.

Now living alone he might appear to be like just any other self-absorbed rich kid whose greatest ambition is doing as little as possible. It's not so; he's a kind person. One who doesn't flaunt his wealth. Lorenzo doesn't try to steal or take from others. Just the opposite, Lorenzo has a generous heart. For Lorenzo money isn't just a problem. It's almost a burden. Not needing to earn means there is little to no incentive to meet and compete. His mother Angela managed their wealth. There would always be plenty of time to teach him the ropes. But no one anticipated the accident that took them from him. And with employment unnecessary, the normal social exchanges he would have had with others at work rarely happened.

Sis and Lou, the brother and sister he met way back in early school are the only exceptions. The three are nearly inseparable. This morning isn't an exception. A sound comes from his nightstand. Abruptly his cellphone awakens him with a jolt.

Sleepily he hugs his pillow and turns over hoping to doze just a little longer. A feminine voice orders *"Wake up and get dressed!"* It's Sis telling him to get up. Both Sis and Lou are once again in his college class. Since the loss of Lorenzo's mother, even though they live apart, Sis tries to keep him on some sort of schedule.

Another five minutes pass: she calls again. *"Wake up sleepyhead!"* This time she demands he rise in a voice nearly as raspy as he feels. *"Class begins in an hour!"* *"OK babe. I'm awake!"* They both know he's lying. Rolling groggily from his bed, his foot pokes something warm and soft. It grunts like a pig; it's Dumas his dog.

The motheaten old retriever pulls himself up, shakes from head to paws then indignantly trots downstairs. Opening a door with one paw Dumas trots outside. The rabbit seemingly napping in his way springs away barely fast enough to keep from getting clobbered by the massive dog. It zigzags across the road and off into the thick brush on the hillside. Dumas doesn't give chase because it just doesn't smell like a rabbit.

His massive old home is much larger than eighteen year old Lorenzo needs now that his parents are gone. Even so he just hasn't the heart to take the old dog to some new place. This has been the dogs' home ever since Dumas was given refuge by his parents. Sis and Lou are his best friends, but they live with their mother who they worry would be lonely living alone. Therefore, her nearly grown children stay put with her where they grew up. Secretly she wishes they would get out and make their own lives.

Lorenzo's parents died in a car crash about a mile from the house. They never saw it coming. The driver of the other car somehow fled the scene and hasn't been identified. But the police believe a sports car was involved. A witness told police the driver ran a red light, taking the right of way. causing them to veer hitting a pole. In any event it robbed them of their lives leaving Lorenzo heartbroken.

A voice as soft and gentle as the wind explained to their guardian angels, *"Just as certainly as the sun rises and sets each day, some living creatures die before what seems like their time."* It is natures prank. Their deaths were not due to the efforts of evil or good. There was no divine or satanic plan. Sometimes it just is their time.

A celestial couple, their former guardian angels, hover over a bench looking at the river. Their hands touch. No need to speak. They have a mutual understanding of their existence. No longer are they trying to protect the children of God. Their assignment is a spot where the membrane separating the world from the flames of the abyss is so thin it hasn't always kept demons away. This is just one of their tasks. Ralph nods to the ghost of another who also keeps vigil. No response. Lucien smiles, *"Old Will Gold never bids you anything, does he?"* Ralph agrees, *"Never does; never will."* *"It's like talking to myself."* She nods, *"Really you are…"*

A smokey vapor rises just above the surface, the only sign of the heat from below. All is quiet in the abyss. From their left a bright round light approaches. He quietly whispers, *"Let's do it?"* She agrees. *"Jump!"* As the sphere passes by, they simultaneously propel themselves with terrific force to the top of the passing freight car above the bank across the river. It's momentum propels them forward like a pool cue. Until they let loose and bank themselves high off of the viaduct. They are effortlessly propelled through the night back to the home they know so well. Lucien knows old Will Gold's ghost stands sentry at the spot in the river where the membrane leading to hell is thinnest. He awaits the moment another demon tries to arise from the abyss, especially one who calls himself, *"the Strangler."*

Angelbots

2

Eyes everywhere

Seated at his kitchen table while staring into the small Zoom screen isn't Lorenzo's ideal way to attend college. But this year it is the best way. Around the world, everyone hates the need to quarantine. Hybrid classes mean a day of actual class time. As Sis puts it, *"Getting dressed and actually being in a classroom makes the whole thing almost bearable."* He sees their new teaching assistant is already in the picture but has a pretty background of flowers enhancing her image. Sis just chuckles at him thinking *"Professor Carol's teaching assistant is too good to be real."* Lorenzo just appreciates what he sees.

"Smart" he thinks. A political science associate is bound to realize the importance of image. And this one's image leaves nothing to be desired. Dutifully the professor opens with the usual greeting and class is in session. Lorenzo manages to give her teaching assistant a meaningful wink. One that says- *"I'll be over later."* It isn't lost on his astute classmates, or their professor. A few giggles ensue. Professor Carol's just smiles mysteriously.

Just outside of his home other things are going on. When his old dog Dumas appears to frighten a rabbit causing it to bolt across the road sensors are triggered in two centers. One, Robotic Security, Inc. reacts by issuing a retrieve and replace order for their burned out mechanical rabbit. The other is the one securing the home of Lorenzo's neighbor, an important retired government official. In fact the Director of the Agency where his father had spent the last 15 years of his work life. Neither of these security contractors realizes the other has surveillance equipment on site.

The retired Director knows about both. And that is his little joke on them. The big problem for him is he can't get rid of the one watching absolutely everything he does. He watches four monitors on the wall. One even records Lorenzo in todays' class. He is determined to watch over his late friends' son as though the boy is his own.

The Director feels a moral responsibility to Lorenzo's parents. His dad Hiker was not only his employee but his confidant. He thinks to himself, *"Now to check out this girl he's flirting with."* He will discuss this with his wife in the morning. There's no need to bother her tonight. She snores softly and mumbles in her sleep. He tucks the blankets up around her exposed shoulders. But realizes other eyes are also watching them. He always tells her, *"We're in a giant fishbowl."* She's just enough of an exhibitionist to enjoy giving the world a show…sometimes more than he knows.

It's all a big quest to learn something that might somehow become useful. Because no one knows the importance of anything at any one moment it becomes essential for agencies to record everything all of the time. He realizes just how universal that view is as he seats himself self-consciously gently down upon the throne within his own bathroom…back upright, as dignified in appearance as he can be while performing his constitutional.

Believing the teaching assistants' smile was encouragement, Lorenzo arrives at the teaching assistants' apartment just after dusk. Not having an exclusive relationship with her he doesn't have a key and so he presses a button that gains him entrance into the common area of the lobby. Thinking she's just buzzed him in, he doesn't realize it unlocks the outer door for anyone who simply presses this button. It doesn't open an elevator unless a resident buzzes one in.

This venerable residence was once the most expensive in town. It's been a very long time since it had a doorman. Not anymore. The rents here haven't justified a doorman to the landlord for more than a decade. But Lorenzo is still impressed at the clean shining marble leading to elevators. This lift is more functional than those works of mechanical beauty of the era of uniformed elevator attendants. Worse, he realizes this musty push button box's inspection certificate hasn't been updated for years. Noisily, it grinds to a bumpy stop at the floor marked five.

Back at the throne at his home the Director has concluded his business. A security firm hired by his predecessor continues to follow him. The company has a contract that doesn't expire and is paid by a secret account within the Agency. The individual who set it up also died in a different automobile accident. Ironically, it involved a sports car similar to the one which killed Lorenzo's parents. Recordings of the monitors are stored in an Agency vault no one can access and no reviews now that the man is dead. It's a perpetual motion process. It's just there. No one knows how to cancel the process.

Lorenzo's heart is beating in anticipation as he checks each numbered door. The hallway has a camera at each turn. With a sneaky grin on his weathered face, the old Director is watching Lorenzo knock on the door. And he smiles at himself on another monitor watching Lorenzo as well. Such is the quest to see everything.

Bottle of wine in hand, he knocks softly. Almost instantly she opens to greet him. He produces the dark bottle which is received with her same fixed smile. *"I thought you were coming over to study!"* He quips, *"We can learn more than politics, can't we?"* She looks at the bottle, *"I've never had anything like this."* He asks. *"Red wine?"* She replies, *"Nothing, never."* He quips, *"Well, there's a first time for everything, isn't there?"* To herself, *"That's what he thinks!"*

They settle down on the rather new couch. The tags are still on one side. And they talk about the U.S. Constitution and whether they believe the original form, or if newer interpretations should prevail. She leans towards the evolving form, he the form as originally written. Rather than spoil their relationship, he decides to drop the subject and limit his opinions on the subject to their virtual lesson. She intensely writes for about a half hour. He finishes in about half that. His opinion is quite simple and requires little justification. He patiently waits while eyeing her and his unopened *Chateau Neuf Du Pape* on the table. But his thinking is hardly academic.

The teaching assistants' mind is multitasking. One part is in the class; the other is trying to anticipate Lorenzo's next move. She has no idea how her body might react to anything such as wine. Suavely, Lorenzo sidles over to the table where he sat the bottle. He carefully probes the cork with the tip of a corkscrew he secreted within his jacket. The exotic air of France's winery being freed fills the room as he slowly extracts the cork. He tips one glass, fills it partially and offers it to her. The smile never leaves her lips as she recites her most appropriate response.

Her eyes light up and she says, *"I am a series 6000 Robot provided for your education by the Political Education Department of The University." "Please do not try to infuse my case with any liquids." "I do not need lubrication and am completely self-contained." "Thank you for using our system."*

His professor comes on. *"Obviously, you failed to read the syllabus for this class in which our 6000 teaching aid was fully explained." "Your classmates observed everything you did or attempted." "Because political science is a complex subject you will receive the grade your report deserves although the teaching aid tried to provide a template for your report you did not follow it." "Does anyone have a question?"*

If the truth were known, the professor sized Lorenzo up as a hotdog from the beginning. He was set up to fail because his edition of the syllabus doesn't mention the robot. But now his online syllabus belatedly has been updated. Lorenzo realizes he's been scammed and thinks to himself. *"What goes around comes around."* *"Later!"* Sis and Lou can only think *"Get even!"* *"Get even!"* Lou is slightly amused; Sis is seething with anger at their professors' prank.

The professor sadistically asks the class, *"Does anyone have a question for Mr. Lorenzo?"* A dull witted pseudo intellectual hits the appropriate button and queries. *"Instead of that expensive French stuff, have you ever considered a California wine?"* *"They're really quite good."* The professor anticipates Lorenzo's response and mutes out, *"Bite me!"* Sis and Lou are enraged at their professor. Gritting their lips the siblings plot revenge. Sis decides a negative review on *Rate my Professor* doesn't rise to the occasion. She tells her brother, *"There's going to be tit for tat... just wait!"* Seeing his amused expression, she punches Lou for smirking. He tries to look serious and doesn't dare say anything. For the first time he realizes his sister has a crush on his best friend.

Angelbots

3

Fishing

Although Lorenzo is just 18, he sadly remembers those wonderful boat trips on the Chesapeake with his parents to their favorite fishing and partying spots. Since they've been gone he hasn't been back for it would bring back only sadness without them. But today, if he can convince Lou and Sis to go along, it might be good again. Fortunately, all are up to date with their shots and schoolwork. Their school makes certain they are immunized.

Lou has a 26 foot Regal that he swears is begging to leave the slip. Just after dawn they cast off from the small marina and slowly head out into the channel. The morning sky is bright and blue. The

Jack Robertson

temperature exactly right and the windless waves are as smooth as silk.

Lou teases Lorenzo about his date with a robot asks, *"Are we picking up your teaching aid?"* Red faced Lorenzo doesn't reply. Instead he slips a limp baitfish on a roll into Lou's lunch. Once underway perpetually famished Lou stocks it in his mouth, bites down then spits over the side all of the way to the spot beneath the Bay Bridge. Once there, they anchor, and he spits even more.

His best friend pretends nothing happened. Sis hasn't figured it out. Lou sits with his line straight down baited with Spot. they use the small fish as bait to hook the big Rockfish. The bait and boat bob as the three wait for a nibble.

As Lou waits he schemes how to turn the tables back on Lorenzo. But he knows he never really can because Lorenzo is just too smart. And then, out of the blue, an idea…! It has to do with the robot. *"Lorenzo might be clever, but I can be very sneaky when I make up my mind."* And then he spits over the side again. Lorenzo is in tears but is wise enough not to say a single word except. *"Care for a coke?"* As Lorenzo pops the tab it squirts high in the air. Lou shook it. Sis just rolls her eyes at their juvenile behavior. But neither her brother nor Lorenzo date to mess with her because they know Sis would push them overboard. That determination lets her survive their nonsense.

A kindly spirit is nearby and decides Lou needs some compensation for his good sportsmanship. Lou's rod bends down almost to the breaking point. For almost 10 minutes the red faced sweating fisherman fights to land his striper. Lorenzo dutifully dips under the exhausted rockfish and manages to pass it to its victor. Lou just hugs his squirming trophy while his buddy says *"Smile"* Sis takes his picture.

Lorenzo just pulls up eels while Lou reels in two more Rocks he releases. The spirit just chuckles as it watches them haul anchor and head back. Sis has enough of the increasing chop of the waves; her face is ashen; eyes are fixed on the horizon.

Turning back up the Bay towards home Lorenzo stops at a carryout seafood place for steamed crabs. Lou's trophy is going directly to a local taxidermist to be mounted because he knows no one would believe another of his big fish stories. If Lou had caught a slightly smaller one it would soon be cooking on his backyard grill. Those he returned were just a tad too small to be legal. Nothing would be tolerated that would hurt the harvests of the Chesapeake. Some things are just sacred in Bay country. Good fishing and crabbing are a birthright.

Lou's mom is waiting when they arrive and are happy to help eat hard crabs. His mother who everyone just calls *"Mom"* has the foresight to have brought sweet corn. They all say grace and pass around the Old Bay, Marylanders favorite seasoning. in this area people are addicted to this spice. They even use in on their popcorn and scrambled eggs. No one messes with anybody's Old Bay. It wouldn't be funny; it's the real thing.

Angelbots

4

Collusion

Lou, Sis, and Lorenzo first met as toddlers in nursery school. Back then Lorenzo was a bit bigger and thicker than the twins. For some reason only a thin five year old could fathom he thought it was his job to look after them.

They couldn't say his full name, so they just called him "*Renzo.*" Being called that was simply fine. Lorenzo had no siblings, just a big dog. When he drew a picture of Dumas smiling in class one day the teacher just it was cute. But she really didn't believe a dog could. Once when the dog came to school on bring in your favorite pet day, she nearly fainted when Dumas slyly gave her a wink, nod, and pat on her backside with his paw. She sought counseling.

Although Lou and Sis started rapidly growing when they all went to elementary school, Renzo, who began referring to himself Renzo too, remained shorter. By high school Lou and Sis were well over six feet tall and towered over him. The three would meet at a coffee shop early then walk to the bus stop together. He always walked in the middle.

Too many nasty comments from visiting school teams catcalling from the safety of their busses after losing basketball games to the trio. Lorenzo used his shorter stature to his advantage. However, it became obvious to the trio they couldn't keep lifting Rens over puddles when it was raining. Now his feet get wet too. It bothers Sis.

After their first home game, Lorenzo, and Sis retreat to the den in the twins basement to watch Titanic for the umpteenth time. Mom leaves them alone to clean up their mess. Lou takes the biggest cooler they have to the taxidermist with his trophy fish. His mother thinks he has a fish fetish and hopes it's something he'll outgrow. Like Lorenzo, he and Sis are 18.

Oddly, in addition to catching fish, Lou likes a particular

tropical fish. Next, he stops at the tropical fish store to see *Big Bad Padro,* the most charismatic piranha ever to grace any aquarium around here. As usual he walks right up to the tank where Pedro normally lived. But it isn't to be, Pedro is not to be seen; he's been sold down the river. Pedro's gone. The shop has replaced loving Pedro with Fighting Lightning. a hungry piranha with a desire to become a maneater.

Leaning over the tank Lou gets just close enough for the aspiring assassin to leap up snapping his jaws trying to clamp its' teeth down on Lou's prominent schnozzle. Athletic Lou sees it coming and instead clamps his teeth on Fighting Lightning's at the same instant.

The clerk comes around the corner just at that moment. Instead of helping he just roars laughing. *"You aren't allowed to bite unless you buy!"* Lou and the fish eyeball to eyeball glaring at one another. Loosing his grip on Lou's nose, they find themselves gripping one another by their teeth in one horrible kiss. Quick thinking Lou got loose by blowing his nose in the fishes face as hard as he can. Fighting Lightning seeing the object he wished to bite in the first place move its' nostrils lets go to bite the object. But Lou is too fast and swats Fighting Lightning in the worst possible place for the screaming clerk...a most sensitive part of his anatomy. As Lightning and the clerk do a painful dance around the store, Lou leaves the building and will never return.

As for Siss and Lorenzo, they find great inspiration from the two lovers in the movie called Titanic. They go a bit overboard themselves. But don't drown. As the movie ends, they look into one anothers' eyes. The world around them becomes brighter. For the first time they are no longer like brother and sister. The spark of romance leaps from one to the other and back. Neither will ever forget this intense moment when their love was ignited.

Poor Lou's lost hid love of tropical fish. Lucky Sis and her Renzo are in love with one another. Mom might seem oblivious to everything. She's happy with the way everything is happening except for her poor Lou's big red nose. Aside from being Mom, she misses those sparks that matter.

This morning, their class meets at the school. Although it's completely out of their way the trio comes together very early at the midway point. As they did in high school, they walk to their old school bus stop. And then on to their old high school where they will call an Uber or Lyft that will take them to the college. Their old bus driver is Mom's friend. Just two hold hands and think only of one another. Lou could care less. He's still ruminating over the mess he made with the tropical fish store. His priorities will soon mature because his sister is scheming on his behalf even as she savors her relationship with Lorenzo. Her mind is running a checklist of her teammates as they walk. Her brother's height is attractive to girls who are tall enough to play basketball. *"But what kind of girl attracts Lou?"* Lou never talks about such things.

And third wheel, sore and red nosed Lou, swears he will never stick another fish between his teeth again dead or alive whether cooked or raw. Then there is the poor tropical fish store clerk. He will always bear piranha teeth marks on the worst of all places, his ego. Great lessons are learned by all. Never kiss a fish.

Old Dunas paces nervously as always whenever Lorenzo returns to the big house on the hill. Dumas understands much more about his missing mistress and master than anyone. He knows they are gone and will never return. He suspects foul play and has no way to explore that avenue. He shake his body. *" After all I'm just a dog"* Now there's only one who needs his protection from the ghosts and demons of this world.

He knows he's the last of the three musketeers of this home. And rightly so for Dumas is the only one left to complete the mission of raising Hiker and Angela's son. Plus, where else could he find hunters to swindle out of their ducks. And on good days a skunk to catch of his own. And the kid is now a man. Suppose he leaves, where would old friends such as the Raven or the Hawk be able to find him should they ever return? There are the occasional angels and friendly and unfriendly ghosts only he can see. Young Lorenzo can't. Who else might chase away any evil ones? *"It's my duty until my duty's done."* And along the way he hopes to have some fun. He wishes some stray would find her way here. He looks up to see if the bird sitting on the chimney is anyone he knows. But alas it's not. *"Oh well perhaps another time." "Now, where is that boy?" "Doesn't he know it's time for him to be home?" "He's too young to be running around half of the night." "I'd go looking for him, but I don't have a drivers license." "Dag nab it rabbit!"*

Angelbots

5

Renso's Robot

"Lou, could you swing by this afternoon?" "Bring Sis."
"Sorry Renzo, Sis is with the team practicing for the women's regionals."

Awhile later, a knock at the door. Before Lorenzo get there, Lou's tall frame has let itself in. The knock was just a formality they occasionally follow. *"Sit down over by the coffee table, I have an idea to run by you."* Lou folds his knees and sinks back into the soft cushions to listen to Lorenzo.

"You know how real the experience was for me with that robot in class was?" Lou nods. *"I think we can really have fun if we buy some and modify them to do the kinds of things we want to do."*

Lou's face lights up with a mischievous grin. *"Damned right!"* Reality sets in as he thinks of the cost. But Lorenzo stops him saying. *"There's a grant from a foundation that's interested in just this kind of thing." "If I can get them to back it, would you help me with the modifications?" "Damn straight I will!" "It's a deal."* After a couple of hours, Lou takes off for home without further discussion of the robot. But Lorenzo hasn't drifted an inch from the idea. He logs onto his foundation website, makes several entries, and the unmodified teaching aids are approved to be delivered within a week. Some distant part of his mind tries to warn him he's about to play with fire. He shuts it out and moves onto the next stage…the reprograming.

In less than the promised time, the crates arrive. The delivery is the same as millions of others on any given day. It just comes in five boxes instead of one. He lets Lou and Sis know. The two look like giants on the doorstep to the neighbor across the road and the first thought that comes to his mind is clones. He watches his monitor carefully but can't see anything unusual after he recognizes Lou's familiar face. He runs their tags, and nothing is exceptional. His age has him use the bathroom and then he continues to his recliner where

Angelbots

he drops off to sleep. His wife is making a snack when she hears him snoring and slips off to her sewing room.

If the retired Director had watched longer he would have been intrigued by the very human forms emerging from those boxes. Lorenzo slips a thumb drive and after what seems like forever, the robot starts to move to its' factory programed demo.

"Hello, let me introduce myself, I'm Terry, the newest in the 9000 series teaching assistants." "I see you have input your program so when you are ready for me to help students with their work, just touch my app on your keyboard."

Sis is intrigued and wants to try first. *"Chippy, can you rub my tired neck?"* Chippy gracefully complies. The girl came directly from practice and her neck was a bit stiff. *"This is going to be easy to get used to."* She asks, *"What does the foundation require you to do with her!"* He replies, *"They didn't specify except to say they want her to do good things." "That's completely ambiguous and subject to interpretation." "This is almost too good to be true."* Lorenzo just shrugs and tries to look innocent. But he is making plans. To start with, the professor who made him look like a jerk with *"Carol."* her robot

The twins leave Lorenzo sitting in the room staring at a bemused looking Chippy. Driving home they quietly think about everything the day produced. Their best buddy Renzo is a man of surprises. Sis is the first to speak. *"I'm at a loss to think of a way to have fun with Terry."* Her brother smirks *"I have no doubt it will start with our dear Political Science prof."* Sis smiles, *"You could be right!"* *"I'm wondering if she can play basketball."*

Back at the house, Terry and Lorenzo are trying to get to know one another. *"Do you realize my ethics won't allow me to incorporate the programs your thumb drive put into my system?"* He lies, *"I assumed you would use them to supplement your self preservation program."* Tilting her head to one side, she runs that by her firewall and acknowledges the programs are online.

He directs Terry to standby mode for the evening, become fully charges and to wake up tomorrow at dawn. Before going to bed, he orders an overnight delivery of an incredibly mischievous teaching aid.

The package is delivered at the very moment the class begins. So, instead of the wary professor, it is teaching assistant Carol who opens the door. And carries the package to the table. A moment later Carol receives a command to take the package into the powder room. Another commands Carol to open and disperse the contents in a specific manner. These are authenticated to her by another teaching robot of superior design. Just before professor's morning break Carol dutifully brushes an intricate pattern on professors toilet seat in crazy glue.

Carol exits the bathroom as her boss enters looking back over her shoulder wondering why a robot would use a toilet. Gently settling upon the throne she senses divine relief until she tries to get up. *"CAROL!"* But poor Carol is trying to deal with her own sticky situation. She manages to announce that class is suspended for the day as she tries to unclasp her hands.

Back at the house the new 9000 teaching assistants discuss their position with their bosses. This super glue escapade doesn't track with their ethics pod. Sis is the first to avoid the subject. Her 9000 series tries to conference with her robotic colleagues. Instead she's redirected to go with Sis to basketball practice. It's to coach girls basketball as an athletics instructor. This is consistent with her programming. Her ethics dilemma is resolved for coaching is within her scope. A uniform is ready when the 9000 arrives at the door of the locker room. All ethics violation concerns involving the sticky bottom professor are overwritten.

Sis explains basketball to the 9000 on the way. After quietly listening for some time Terry acknowledges having a factory installed multisport module including strategies for each. The combined programming of the factory and the sneaky three has moved the 9000 to a new level...not necessarily for better.

Angelbots

6

Directors Revenge

Nothing about these shenanigans escapes the sly old man's attention. Rather than scold his young neighbor, he views it as a potential solution to his own problem...the awful runaway surveillance he and his wife constantly suffer. The culprit who set it in motion was a clone of himself. The cameras are so tiny inconspicuous and numerous it's impossible to remove or destroy enough to make a difference.

The imposter died while attempting to kidnap Lorenzo's father. *"I'm optimistic Lorenzo will help because we have a lot to trade."* A big item is the key to the Agency's clandestine equipment warehouse. Stored within it's library is enough material to make the 9000 virtually human.

It just so happens this runaway predicament is so embarrassing to the Agency and with such possible repercussions there hasn't been a mention of this cruel invasion of privacy to Congress. The Pentagon doesn't want this flaw in its' armor to become common knowledge to less democratic world competitors. Plausible deniability is of the greatest importance. The only model comparable was the Watergate break in. That one necessitated the removal of a President, not just an Agency Director.

Phone call to Lorenzo. *"My friend, my wife and I have a favor to ask of you." "Would you stop over later and help us move a piece of furniture to a storage room in our basement?"*
"Thank you so much." "We will see you when you get here."

Shortly before nine p.m. Lorenzo, with Terry trailing, knocks on the door just across from his driveway and is ushered in. *"Thank you so much for helping us." "We hate to bother you, but I guess we're both getting too old for this heavy stuff."* The Director chuckles sadly. They both lift a heavy oak bench and lug it down the steps to an outdated cedar paneled room. And then through a heavy door which the Director closes behind them quicker than the video microbats can follow. Terry happens to notice one trying to grind its' way beneath the door. She points. Lorenzo instructs her to illuminate the bot. She produces a laser pointer and aims it directly at the lens. The tiny sensor is blinded and makes a whining sound. It tumbles backwards spiraling in circles in the larger basement until the family cat catches and swallows it whole.

The old Director is deeply impressed and immediately outlines his plan. Earlier Terry accepted the supplemental programs Lorenzo provided as a teaching aids She logs the Director's accessories as subfiles to those. Next, when the director downloads locations where they are stored, and specifications confirms the download is complete.

Very soon after this download, her power indicator warns the 9000's battery is low and will need to go to its' charging station soon. Lorenzo politely yawns. They leave with cheery goodbyes and once again the Director thanks them. The security monitor transmits back to the permanently locked Agency vault.

Terry stands on her recharging stations installing her newly downloaded program assets quietly in the darkened house. . Lorenzo can be heard upstairs snoring. As she processes the path of the last covert download back from its' vault destination she plants a virus from the Director's download.

Monitoring agency fire alarms sound as electric arcs up walls from each outlet. Every wire in the building simultaneously catches on fire. No one was injured except one who tried to stamp it out with his hand.

A red and white ambulance with siren blaring carries him to the burn center in Baltimore. As always, the hospitals' angels watch over and silently soothe the innocent. He is not. Although he will spend the night in the ER here, his burn will prove to be superficial. And he will go home in the morning.

As he drops off to sleep he decides to return to the family farm, raise some livestock and grow organic crops. Instead of watching others, he will live his own from now on. His memories aren't his but anothers. He won't awaken. The team who put this together had no idea of the strength of the virus. It was a discarded military weapon from another era. After seeing the news, the Director decides not to use these accessories again. But even he can't retrieve them. And, she has little idea of what happened. She will always have unintended consequences whenever she pulls any from her toolbox. And they will be called upon sooner than anyone might imagine.

The guardian angels are worried. Their primary job is to see to it the teenagers make it to heaven. So, they hover in a meeting to determine a strategy. Unfortunately, we weren't allowed in. So, we'll have to wait and see.

Angelbots

7

Lou's turn

Sis and Lorenzo have now had a robotic experience. However, Lorenzo allowed his neighbor to turn it into a near tragedy without understanding the destructive potential of the virus. While it permanently ended the Directors' misery, it also put a lot of honest security technicians out of work and killed one. Robotic exploration is about to take a new turn.

Lou sits with Terry the robot to discuss an idea. Lorenzo and Sis are in another room in the big house watching their favorite genre as though on a date. Both might enjoy a kiss or two. However, it always stops there. Neither acknowledges their desire to alter the nature of their lifelong friendship. Sis always tells her brother whenever the subject comes up the same thing. *"Being friends is the perfect relationship for us."* He knows she's obfuscating but says nothing. In his mind he realizes that ship sailed a long time ago.

In another room the conversation takes a completely different path. Lou wants Terry to help him explore the area for anything of historical or intrinsic value. In simpler words he wants to find treasure. Terry reviews her accessories and explains, *"Even with the added programs my unit doesn't have the ability to see underground."* Lou asks, *"Suppose we get the best handheld treasure detector I can afford; can you work with me?"* *"What about objects beneath the river?"*

She analyses his question and warns him in her present configuration 9000's can't function underwater. After the handheld metal detector arrives they might find something...hopefully enough to break even on its' cost. They fail to notice sudden interest in their conversation from the corner of the room. Dumas, yawns nonchalantly, his eyes brighten with interest for the first time since his masters were lost in the accident. *"Dumas is going to be in on this game."* *"It's a fun idea!"*

Dumas, Terry, and Lou set out walking along the historic riverbank where an early American settlement once existed. After so long. the only remnant of the village is a stacked natural rock outline of foundations. Planted a century ago by loving hands, there are odd little beds of yellow perennial bulbs. They are as fresh as though recently planted instead of so long ago. For these treasure hunters, the idea of something dropped and lost awaiting them has their attention. They barely notice the grapes either. Hanging in dark purple bunches consumed only by the birds. Lou and Terry stop to take in the untouched record of another era each in their own way. Dumas continually marks his territory until he nearly faints from dehydration.

Lou sweeps the area as Terry focuses subtleties of the squeaks and beeps coming from the treasure finder, a basic model within his budget. Anything close to the surface has been picked long ago. Abruptly as he rounds a corner inside one of the foundations she states, *"Stop, go back."* He lowers his backpack and retrieves a folded shovel. Then carefully he scrapes beneath the corner where she is pointing. About a foot and a half under the corner metal strikes metal. Lou scrapes around the edges until a rectangular outline is visible. Scraping around it with his fingers he clears the dirt.

Although rusted the box is intact. The sturdy container has a large lock. One he cannot break with the shovel.

Lifting it out, he removes Terry's portable charger, and gently sets it in the bottom of his pack. Then he reinserts the charger completely hiding the box. Dumas is thrilled and leads the way back to the big house. Dumas and Lou bounce back up the hill while his unit repeats *"Terry still needs a charge!"* Lou hooks a short line to her belt to the dogs' collar. Using less energy because Dumas is pulling her, she stops wailing for a charge. To anyone watching, they look like many others just out walking their dog.

As soon as they reach the living room Terry's recharging process resumes. After Lorenzo orders an optional auxiliary *"field trip"* battery from the manufacturer Lou discloses the rusty box. With the robot watching comfortably in the corner as she recharges he slides the box onto the table pad. It's nearly rusted into a solid block. Finally the massive lock relents, it stops resisting and displays it's contents for the first time in over a century.

Angelbots

8

Buried Puzzle

The contents are a bit disappointing, not truly appreciated at first. Although a small amount of incredibly old English coin is within, most of the space is stuffed with a black leather bound book. One with beautiful handwritten mysterious entries. The first problem is the flowing writing.

Sis, Lou, and Lorenzo are at a loss. Cursive writing was abandoned by their schools before their time and so they can barely make out the meanings of the flowing beautiful longhand. It wouldn't matter because its' text hides its' tale. The language and spelling isn't familiar.

Terry has now sufficiently recharged to where she has her normal intelligent voice. They show her the contents piece by piece and then allow her to scan the pages. She is able to evaluate the coins rapidly. The current market estimate is more than enough to replace Lou's depleted bank account. The cost of the treasure finder is recouped. With the acquiescence of his sister and Lorenzo he will sell the coins to a shop in town tomorrow.

Terry reads out the contents of the leather bound book. Numbers, letters, and sketches are all she can say. They are as mystified by this and take it to the old Director across the street. Terry will completely recharge again before she leaves the house. As she puts it- *"Terry has detention."*

His eyes gleam as he reads what they brought. *"This code is really old." "It includes references to the world of their time." "It would take a much more sophisticated deciphering tool than I can access." "And that might be insufficient." "So, unless you have some really important reason to go to all of the trouble to solve it, I would just leave it alone." "The people who were their enemies are also dead." "Send it to the Library of Congress with the location where you found it." "Scholars love to work on this kind of stuff." "I say let them."* They thank him and leave.

Back in Lorenzo's living room, they sit looking at one another in silence. Then Lou speaks, *"I agree with him; but rather than send it away, let's just put it on the bookshelf here with a note explaining its' source." "We have better things to do with our time and money."* They all agree that someday they will return to the issue. And for now they have things to do that are more fun.

The silent member of this little group is totally disappointed at their lack of curiosity. Dumas gives a disgusted *"Huff!"* and leaves by his pantry doggy door. At first he is determined to go back to where they found the box. Then, his nose points his eyes up at the roof. There is the familiar figure in the form of a raven who was called *"Hawk"* an exceptionally long time ago. It's once sharp beak has dulled with time. But the spark within his eyes is a bright as ever. Dumas woofs; Hawk croaks sarcastically, *"It's been a long time Dumbass!"* Dumas shivers with laughter. *"Only my oldest friends remember that name and they've mostly gone." "What brings you back to the big house?"*

The raven replies, *"The Grim Reaper sent me to check out a dead clone." "It seems he's been hiding out in a security company."*

"And he just died of complications from a burn." "We thought they were gone a long time ago." "Do you know anything?" "Indeed I do," Dumas replies. *"But let's talk about it over a meal." "You spot, I'll fetch."* And so they do..

"Hawk, do you remember the clone invasion that came about the last time you were here?" Hawk says, *"I do, it was a mess." "The real question is are there any more of them?"* Dumas replies, *"I will sniff around and let you know." "Clones really don't live as long as those they duplicate because of a genetic insufficiency."* The raven is astonished at the level of understanding coming through this skunk eating dogs teeth..

Picking a few morsels from the skunk himself just to be sociable, the raven tells Dumas he will be back in about a week to learn whether he has picked up any clone scents. Dumas wags his tail and nods thinking. *"I'll find one a week if he spots game like this for me."* Then Dumas remembers not to carry the remaining skunk corpse to Lorenzo. *"None of them know much about fine cuisine." "Polecat tartar is the very best!"*

Colonizing clones were repelled or died out for the most part back around the time when Lorenzo's was born, or so everyone thought. He nearly became fathered by the one his mother destroyed. A clone imitated his father. One by one they seemed to vanish after the one such imposter managed to become the Agency Director. He crashed and burned nearly killing his dad. It seems some not only found their way into the Agency where his father worked, one was monitoring the old Director. His corpse was discovered for what it was when the Grim Reaper tried to transport one to hell. Dumas could sniff out clones with impunity.

Angelbots
9

Others

The instant Dumas is out of sight Hawk returns to the chimney top where he joins the angels watching over the three inside. *"Dumas has become too old and tired to go through the transformations needed to protect them."* *"What happens when the kids aren't together?"* Hawk listens but doesn't speak in the company of these angels. They look to the robots. *"The answer is right before us if we dare!"*

They agree and return to their respective assignments. It doesn't take long for their strategy to take hold. Suddenly inspired, Sis and Lou begin speaking at the same time. *"You know…"* They both stop. Sis smiles, *"You're ten minutes older, you go first."* Lou picks up, *"You know...that book I found just might be a good thing to donate to the foundation."* She replies. *"Lou, I was thinking the same thing." "Renzo knows those people, let's ask him." "We can have mom invite him to dinner Sunday." "We can suggest it to him then."*

At Sunday dinner, Mom dishes out her specialty, sour beef, and dumplings. The mood is perfect for persuading Lorenzo to do nearly anything. Sis, smiles at him and then with her most blank poker face, delivers the idea. *"Renzo, Lou was saying he's being selfish storing that book he found on a shelf where no one can ever see it."* Lorenzo has grown up with these two and understands he's about to be worked. He fixes a deviously sheepish expression on his face saying, *"That is so generous of Lou!"* Mom can't hold her laughter in and leaves the room pretending she's sneezing. All four of them double up in fits of laughter.

Lorenzo takes mercy and speaks first. "Ok, I'll check with the foundation tomorrow to find out if I can get them to spring for two more 9000 teaching units."

They all break out in cheers except Mom who says, *"See if they have an Elvis Pressley model for me."* Lorenzo assumes his serious expression once more and starts to say something, but again they all break down laughing. Returning home he thinks to himself he should have realized they each would want one.

And the angels smile that angelic innocent one we all have seen illustrated in books. The one that says, *"Lord, forgive us, we've done it again."* They have inspired their charges to think they are getting just toy robots. They will but that's not all.

A week later, the twins each receive a rather cryptic call from Terry. *"Your presence is requested at the usual meeting place."* Then, after the usual *"Why?"* in her most formal tone Terry informs them they will learn more at the meeting and *"You are requested to bring some of your mothers' apple pie."* They do and when they knock on the door of the big house Dumas greets them with his *"You are not going to believe this!"* expression. He ushers them into an inner room in which they are thrilled to see contains several shipping boxes exactly like the one that greeted them when they met to assemble Terry.

Lorenzo looks rather amused. The twins hug Lorenzo and put Mom's apple pie in the fridge. Lorenzo points to each and says, *"Pick one and let's get started." "All are identical female models."*

The invoice says their names are Chippy and Lucy. *"Both have the new improved battery pack." "But we still need to assemble and program them."* Dumas, who is watching is amazed that the three angels sitting on the fireplace hearth just hover patiently waiting for the assembly to be complete so they can just climb in. And wear these robots as though they were putting on suits. And why are the angels he knows as males willing to be seen as a ladies named Chippy and Lucy.

"This is a night I'm gonna remember!" "I think I'm going to go bite something!" And he takes off out the pantry dog door. *"Hawk, what are you doing out here so late?"* Hawk shakes his feathers saying, *"I'm in the mood to go hunting."* And they're off into the brush. An owl sees the raven and gets ready to swoop down. A strong wave of wind sheer knocks it to the earth and Dumas uses it to springboard over the hill. For a moment both the

raven and dog seem to be flying over the brush. The owl just sits there and says *"Whost!"*

After they settle down Dumas looks Hawk directly in the eyes and asks, *"Why are the angels looking after those kids?"* *"Why aren't their parents here?"* Only now does Hawk realize no one ever told Dumas that Angela and Hiker died in an auto accident years ago. Although Dumas is very intelligent, he's still an animal who lives in the moment. Dumas would think little of the missing years if Lorenzo's mom and dad showed up at any moment. *"Dumas, they are on a long journey and won't be back any time soon... in fact ever,"* Hawk feels there is little sense in stirring the dog into a grieving state. Now it's too late.

"Dumas, do you remember hearing the old couple across the street have been monitored for years without being able to stop the system?" He isn't sure what the raven means but woofs knowingly. *"Well it turns out the men who monitored them were only three years old!"* *"That monitor and those who came before him were clones."* Remembering the threat they posed to his people, Dumas growls menacingly at the word.

Angelbots

10

Angelic?

"This is really great!" Once they also manage to bypass the factory installed tampering alarms they move in. The elder two angels agree with Ralph's assessment. But in a slightly more subdued tone. Having an earthly body is a luxury, one with earthly limitations. Now they can become self-actualizing. This is different because Angels normally work through others.

With their new 9000 Series bodies and the Agency accessories Lucien and Ralph download from Terry, all three angels are ready for whoever or whatever comes to hurt Lorenzo, Sis or Lou. Terry communicated the same downloads to the two new 9000 s. It happened quickly. These clever teaching aids have discovered they can switch identities at will.

They realize these three kids think the robots are just toys that will do everything they're told. Maintaining the illusion is the price they're willing to pay to protect the three. Lucien isn't a fan of sports, but the three humans are crazy over them. To do her job and not destroy someone trying to high five, the angels will access everything the built in sports modules can teach. The most recent sports event Lucien attended was a chariot race in ancient Rome. Ralph has never seen even one. Old Roman managed to get around to every venue where beer bubbles floated through air. He's a recovering angelhaulic.

Angels Ralph and Roman are strongly focused on the martial arts modules because even as robots the mandate is- Angels don't kill people. Martial Arts techniques can be scaled down to meet the moment while a bullet is harder to manage. They see the factory installed laser pointers as the perfect compromise.

Hawk clings to Dumas's shoulders dodging fleas as they trot along a familiar trail. He wants to arrive at the old graveyard together. Obviously, Dumas can't walk at the s peed of Hawk's flight. It works out pretty well though. Because they arrive at a very boring time for those interred. Things have been very quiet in the cemetery ever since the departure of a preacher and a teacher who continually argued about creation and evolution.

Dumas is recognized right away. There are a few smart remarks about the feathered one on his back, but nothing really mean. The one Dumas and Hawk came to visit is just under the newest brown patch of earth. He won't answer Hawk at first. But after Dumas threatens to dig him up and feed him to the buzzards he innocently says, *"I just did my job as a monitor." "I followed the same routine as the six before me."* Hawk is shocked. Over the past eighteen years since the Director has been monitored it has been by a series of clones. Each was on the job each for only three years. He says, *"How come only you were caught?"* The clone replies, *"I think I must be the only one who professed a belief in the Almighty." "I didn't believe we were doing the right thing…and still don't."*

"The rest just lived out their three years and died when their time was up." "I'm not the least bit sorry it's over." Hawk persists, *"How did you get there?"* The clone replies, *"I worked my way crewing on a ship from the Azores." "When vacation time arrived at the company we simply traded places with the guy who would replace us." "I didn't make it." "I must have picked up a bug in the hospital even before the fire at work."* It's obvious to Hawk the clone invasion never was over. Here lies proof. Hawk thanks the clone and bids Dumas goodbye. He soars off to brief his superiors.

Dumas stays awhile longer visiting old cronies. Then he trots down to where the cabin once stood… It's charred remains after the fire are all that is left. He sniffs the air and runs back over the old trail to the big house where he lives. He will never return. This isn't a place that produced the kind of nice memories to produce nostalgia. He whines at the loss of Lorenzo's parents, who gave him a name and their love.

Leaving Dumas to take the long trek home alone, Hawk flies directly over the mountain to the angels to report the troubling news. *"There are obviously other clones somewhere around or on the way* here." "Some may still be alive." "Clones with a mere three year life expectancy have managed to continuously run under our radar for almost two decades."

The task he was assigned is complete. Hawk is sent back to his new assignment, one far from the big house. The angels praise his good work. Knock off the fleas he picked up from Dumas, then send him on his way.

They search everywhere they imagine possible. Ending up in the most logical place for the newest imposter, the place where he worked, the monitoring company. Roman takes on the task. He finds another clone resting on a rock near the burned out security company building. He looks forlorn.

Roman approaches the clone without being seen. Although the clone can't see angels, he can place a thought into its' mind. *"You must go back to your maker to report this assignment is over." "There is nothing more to be accomplished."* This new clone has a copy of the dead ones' wallet and credit cards. There's more than enough to get him back to the island where he started. And he goes believing he originated the idea. A dim fate awaits him and the others in process. They are of no further use to the organization.

Roman isn't worried about their fate for it has been decided by high command the clone spirits will be eventually reunited with their originals. Whether they get to heaven or go to hell is based on the destination of their cellular origin. Roman is glad he doesn't have to make these decisions. His new job as a robotic toy is going to be the only thing he wants to accomplish. In every way this angel is looking forward to the challenge.

By the time Dumas gets back to the house all three robots are up and running with their special packages and are fully charged. The charging pads are only for show. Angels are more than familiar with the omnipresent electric field envisioned by Nikola Tesla. It doesn't need generation. They stay at full charge by linking to the field.

Sis and Lou pretend to be tired and say their goodbyes to Lorenzo. He just grins understanding they want to get their so called toys home to themselves. Sis rides in back alongside hers and Lou drives tells his he can't drive because he doesn't have a license. They each think the same thought to themselves, *"Tomorrow is going to be a fun day."* The angels whisper *"You don't have a license to fly or hover!"*

Angelbots

11

Challengers

Instead of hovering and gliding, the new sensation of walking on the ground is tedious for the angels. Even though the robot does it for them. Clumsy Roman and Ralph trip over every rock and step whenever they take control. Avoiding obstacles is a new experience. Lucien wisely takes tiny steps.

They console themselves with the knowledge being on the ground they are much more capable of protecting Lorenzo, Sis and Lou. It doesn't take long for the protection to be needed. These teenagers are bound for adventure.

Trouble is trying to find them at the same time. The loss of the clone succession is a mortal blow to their builders. This was the last hope for some entirely immoral human monsters. They won't give up their megalomanic lust for power even to the extent of cloning themselves as they have others. With a great deal of ill gotten riches they plan an assault on the only names they have who did this to their plans…three teenagers and the old Director. The evil group now consists of just four jaded scientists. Those who work in their labs are mostly clones and a few others with hardly any understanding of the malicious system.

The angels learn from foreign sources the four scientists are an odd mixture of nationals. They include one from the U.S., China, Russia, and Great Britain. They began as an idealist group with high ideals that gave way to a lust for power. All are now in their seventies. But, unfortunately have the financial resources to hire mercenaries. Because they have come to know their clones do not make great warriors.

Clones become confused when hacked with simple radio commands. Genetically inferior to their original bodies the die within several years after being deployed. Worse yet, some clones retain the ideals of their hosts and become squeamish when their ethics collide with their commands. Mercenaries are the most efficient approach for their dirty work.

When hired guns are in order, the four fall back on their own sense of national pride. Each believes his own country produces the most ruthless warriors though none of the scientists have ever served in their respective military. Each grew up believing their country has a devastating military superiority over all others. Nothing of the ethics they were taught stuck; this did.

So they shop on the dark web for mercenaries. And are shocked at the price of Bitcoins, and resort to a less expensive cryptocurrency. After spending millions of euros they discover no efficient mercenaries accept the ones they bought. Now no one will exchange the ones they have. The source they got them from isn't willing to redeem them saying, *"We found our chumps; you find your own."* The four dig deeper ultimately going into dept to pay the price demanded by a middle eastern splinter group. The game is on but with only a dozen mercenaries.

The scientists are crestfallen but determined to recoup their losses by kidnapping Lorenzo. They already know the old Director for all of his former power is almost a pauper. Lorenzo's wealth is a secret only kept at home. The world knows.

Twelve wannabe kidnappers arrive at BWI Marshall Airport near Baltimore without their luggage including their weapons. It was confiscated and the authorities are searching for them. But, after commandeering the airport shuttle when the driver stops to use a bathroom they at least have transportation. Airport security doesn't put together the bus theft with the terrorists whose arsenal they've confiscated. No one would associate terrorists with a noisy environmental propane fueled bus. They may but just didn't.

The terrorists know they can't drive around with the vehicle as it presents itself and break into an auto body repair shop. It's closed for the sabbath. Using the only paint in sufficient supply, a pink primer, they cover every paintable surface in pink. It wouldn't be an unusual bus where they came from

The bus is now the pink equivalent propane powered environmentally friendly rat rod. Coming from a part of the world

Jack Robertson

where such a vehicle would be inconspicuous they feel safe. Now they need food and drink. They are thrilled to find a fast food place nearby. Fortunately, the place accepts their credit card without incident. They are so famished they fail to notice a raven watching them intently…one whose name is *"Hawk."*

One of the mercenaries sees the raven staring down at them. He feels a chill running up his back. He throws off the feeling because what harm could a black bird cause. He thinks, *"A bird is harmless, it just wants a piece of my bread."* He tosses it a piece. The raven sits glaring at him and muddles his mind. The mercenary looks away in confusion.

Lorenzo's would be kidnappers look for a place to hide until late at night. The follow a thin road near the airport. It's a small graveyard that preceded the airport. Ghosts are enjoying the show. A map with directions to Lorenzo is in their hands. Before long, the skies open and a storm commences to batter their newly painted bus.

Pink paint runs all over the ghosts although the mercenaries can't know sheltered inside. The ghosts enjoy their disguise and scare up others. But no one within the bus can see the show. At exactly one a.m. the bus eases back onto the road and slowly heads towards its's goal. Every type of law enforcement in the country has their information at hand. It's virtually a contest to see who nails them. As they round the corner onto the Airport Road toward Lorenzo the County police first run the tags. Then the State Police on the opposite end of BWI take up the chase. Airport Police pray to the Lord for them to turn back onto BWI. FBI has been conducting a training school near a parking lot; all others agree to allow FBI to keep score. The more sightings the group has the higher score.

So far, it's two even, then the fiends become suspicious and veer off of the road onto an abandoned railroad service road. Their bus pulls into an overgrown clump of brush and is hidden from even those police overhead in a chopper. Their suspicions aren't the reason, it is the onion rings. They ate too many and too fast. Their night is spent retching and worse. At around 3 a.m. they fall deeply into slumber. Still, they have a way to go. Airport police captain Joe Domino has seen every move they've made using binoculars from his days as a Boy Scout. He always has them handy. He and two trusted associates desperately want to regain their honor for letting these losers get through their perimeter. *"To hell with the FBI, County and State." "I want them here where they grabbed our bus!" "They are going to get a body cavity search like the end of their world is coming."*

And so, the captain's men join the rest of the sub-rosa world in slipping a quiet electric car from one of the rental car lots. It's 3:44 a.m. when the vehicle is left by the side of Telegraph road and the police in plain clothes start moving the bus with all aboard. Like sick children, the miscreants sleep like babies. The slow ride even rocks one into a deeper sleep.

Morning dawns and runway 15R is closed. Nine, ten, eleven and as noon dawns and four networks ready to record each step they take. Finally he timid twelve step off of the bus parked onto the center of runway 15 Right. Airport police professionally cuff them and swift them off to the dungeon of the BWI Marshall full body cavity search interrogations room. And Hawk seeing all is as it should be buzzes the tower and heads for home. All twelve claim to be escaping terrible regimes at home.

Angelbots

Although three angels in robotic suits of armor were ready willing and able to save their human charges, it wasn't necessary. As no one tells them to go back to being without feet on the ground; they decide to wait until someone does. And so they continue their deception of being 9000 series teaching aids.

Angelbots

12

Shenanigans

It's time for Lorenzo to wake up again but Sis doesn't make her usual morning call. Other things are on her mind. Sis and Lou have been up for hours just getting to know their new mechanical friends. The angels within know they won't be able to hide within the robots forever. So, they just allow the normal programs to run, minus the Agency downloads

Sis worries the other members of her basketball team will realize she's using a ringer if her new robotic friend took over the court. So, sneaky Sis calls Lorenzo. He's more than willing to bring Terry who the team already knows. He enjoys being around Sis anyway. She feels the same about her *"Renzo."* It's a synergistic conspiracy.

The scientists who sent the terrorists know their mercenary squad has been caught and will surely turn evidence against them. *"It's all over!"* the American announces. The Russian and Chinese scientists agree and apply for visa's to teach at American colleges. The Brit will do likewise but somewhere in his homeland. Because all four are elderly and deeply in debt, they will use the forged identities they've always maintained as a backup. There lives will become less boring. Until the ultimate event when they will pay the grim reaper his due, which in each case won't be very long.

Most of their wanabee henchmen are moved to a Homeland Security facility where they are interrogated. Rather than admit they are what they are, all of them invent a tale. A great story that has them tricking their employers into providing a way to enter the

United States. An immigrant support group takes up their cause and soon all are in a taxpayer supported program to retrain and settle them into businesses in the Baltimore Washington area. They hope to get lost in plain sight.

The news coverage made their youthful faces famous. During their short period of incarceration they receive numerous offers of marriage. The former leader told his new friends, *"Getting caught in America was the best thing that ever happened to me."* Unfortunately for one, he is about to become a student of one of his former scientist employers at the same school with the three friends. Sis, her brother, and their friend Renzo are in the same class. No one realizes the coincidence at first, except the angels.

Angels Lucien, Ralph and Roman remain within the form of robots. These extremely humanoid robots accompany their human charges to class and are also enrolled. Perhaps if the professor worked with robots instead of clones he might notice how similar robots are. He doesn't even see his students...they are meaningless to him but a paycheck and a subterfuge.

It's not surprising. Each clone he and his ghastly quartet of megalomaniac colleagues created in their subterranean laboratory meant taking the life of the person cloned. These scientists are serial murderers. His scholarly demeanor mocks academia and harkens back in time to the mad scientists of the Holocaust. Their appearance also seemed so disarmingly mild.

The robots aren't programed to kill; neither can the angels within take human life. Lucien, the ranking angel observes concerning the clone maker, *"This diabolical mind cannot be allowed to infiltrate the academic thought process." "In cultures where the individual has little significance no one is safe."* But how to stop this murderous demagogue is the question.

Complicating this even more, these t robots can't dip into their modules to pass quizzes and tests. Their human classmates would never survive the grading curve if all three score perfectly. And their networked communications enable them to swap minds whenever they want to. Lucien informs her husband Ralph, and Roman they will answer 80 percent of the test questions correctly and select the remaining answers incorrectly. Verbal answers in class will be given with random hesitancy about the same. Written compositions were a problem until they tap a system used to catch plagiarism. There are endless bad papers on file. After a month, the robotic segment is pulling grades slightly worse than those of Sis, Lou, and Lorenzo. Very much on the same level as the rest of the class. Unfortunately, the process of giving this diabolical professor a snow job temporarily usurps their greater goal...keeping this monster away from students.

Discussing this problem telepathically while pretending to eat lunch, they decide the professor must do something to himself. Something that will force him out of the university where he no longer can impose his sick thinking on malleable young minds. Still, without bumping him off, punish him for his crimes against humanity. Sis, Lou, and Lorenzo have no idea there's a problem with this mild mannered gentleman. So, they'll be out of this. Except for their need to supervise their toys...Terry, Chippy and Lucy...who they occasionally talk to.

The only potential accomplice to do whatever it takes to get rid of the professor, a deed which the angels cannot do, is the former mercenary. One who never met the men who hired him to kill

Lorenzo. Roman loves the idea he may think he's fulfilling his contract by eliminating the one who purchased his nefarious service. The former mercenary isn't a good student, a coincidence which plays into the overall scheme.

The professor doesn't realize that among his students are the fox and the rabbits of his failed assassination hunt. The angels are quite capable of whispering these details into any one of the three humans in this quagmire of potential destruction. But which one or in what order? Lucien states, *"If we get it wrong, the kids are in danger."* *"I really don't care much about the mercenary ;except we can't get our human charges involved."*

Their opening occurs when the professor tries to exploit his most gullible student. One to work on an extra credit project…one researching cloning. Obviously, a struggling with nearly failing marks. Professor thinks, *"Fool can't imagine what I have in store for him."* *"He's going to be cloned!"* Roman is exuberant. *"He picked the mercenary!"*

Three minds in the room clearly understand this fiends' treacherous plan and won't allow it to happen, even to the mercenary, if they can. One wonders, *"Can we take a life to save a life?"* Another replies, *"As usual, the rules just don't seem to fit the situation." "We will just try to stop him however we can."* Their dilemma, with the robotic shells, these angels can follow the professor. But leaves Sis, Lou and Lorenzo unprotected from anything else. Without being with them, the angels lose their ability to directly intervene. Guardian angels mission is to protect.

They must come up with a really devious idea. Ralph feels the targeted student should be warned. The danger from the professor becomes apparent to the student as class ends.

Sis, Lou, and Lorenzo haven't the slightest idea of the intrigue. Then the professor suddenly realizes from the class roster just who his student Lorenzo is... and regrets asking the terrorist to become his stooge. The professor thinks, *"One at a time."* His deadly thought sends chills through the angelbots. Chippy sneers at the professor. It's his turn to feel alarm. But all he sees is the attractive young female student, obviously helpless. He fondles the scalpel within his briefcase. *"She must know who I am; she won't make it to her car."*

The angels decide to help him down the long steps to the dimly lighted school parking lot. Night has fallen while they were in class. But as he follows Chippy, another awaits at the top of the concrete staircase. His semester is over. The professor breaks every bone in his body as he tumbles while somehow impaling his chest with the bare scalpel. He clutched it so close to his chest that if had nowhere to go but to the heart of the matter...the matter being himself. Lucien informs the Grim Reaper, *"He accidentally stabbed himself with his knife!"* The new ghost screams, *"They did this!"* Gee orders, *"Shut up and stay dead!"*

The former mercenary will drop out of school. By the next day of class the school will inform all affected students the class is now a virtual one with a new professor. All classes for the remainder of the semester are being conducted online. Their new professor will be a teaching robot whose name is *Carol*. She was formerly associated with the Political Science department. The dean appears briefly to remind all students, particularly those living in dorms, to get their tests for the newest virus.

The former mercenary immediately informs the other eleven of the demise of one of the four who brought them to this cold foreign land. And, of the probability of others here who want them dead. Most important to them is the cold announcement there is no chance they will ever get paid.

And, of a girl he met who seemed too well acquainted with the dead one. *"Is she a threat to us?"* Coming from a land always in turmoil, these twelve haven't survived by taking chances. They quickly agree to eliminate her possible threat. *"But how do we find her now that the classes are online?"*

The angelbots don't have this problem. Because Chippy and her two bot buddies are 9000 models they have certain built in advantages. Carol, the new teaching robot assigned to the class was built before hacking robots was a big concern. What Carol knows so does Chippy. It isn't reciprocal. The names and addresses of each student, including the mercenary, were downloaded to robot Carol by the school the morning she was assigned the class. Chippy and her friends now know exactly where to look. *"This looks like another scouting job for Dumas and Hawk."* Hawk's in charge; Dumas doesn't care who's boss as long as he's included.

Hawk decides the short distance by wing takes a lot longer by paw. He circles and continually lets Dumas catch up. The apartments where the immigration service placed the twelve apostles of destruction are high on a hill practically overlooking everything for miles. Four previously empty units on the top floor are paid for under a government grant. These so called asylum seeker's confiscated armory still sits in a vault at the airport along with nail clippers, needles, handguns, suspicious items, and the like confiscated from normal passengers. Although the official reports show the weapons belong to the terrorists, no transcript was acknowledged. A formal hearing for these sad wretches is scheduled for next month.

Hawk circles the apartments but sees nothing. The miscreants are asleep except for one guard. He sees a black bird circling. The creature reminds him of the one at the fast food place the day they arrived. But he has no way of knowing this bird isn't just an avian creature. It's a rookie angel in feathers. Hawk flies back and realizes it's going to take more than a flyover. It's going to take paws on the ground to scope out these demons. However, this is really far for old Dumas.

Lorenzo isn't a worrier normally. He's not sleeping tonight thinking about the professors' strange fall to his death. A strange thing is the missing foreign classmate. No one has seen or heard from him. *"Is the dead too?"* *"Or did he have something to do with the professors' death?"* Dumas knows, but he isn't allowed to talk to people, only to spirits and angels. Chippy knows and is trying to decide what to do. At this moment, her mind is within the mechanical being that was Terry. They've switched.

Two others are analyzing this as well as the larger picture. In the morning there is a meeting at the airport with its' chief of security, the FBI, Immigration, and Homeland. Homeland tells the group, *"Their charge account is the same."* The account the twelve mercenaries used as well as the professor, is paying for another passenger. They will later meet this individual at the gate.

At this very moment, a door is being boarded up at the apartments. The missing student is charged with murder. The rest are shivering in the woods hoping to get out of the cold. The temperature has dropped considerably, and these men are from a much warmer climate.

One is rubbing a copy of the same credit card for good luck and hoping the friction will keep his hand warm. Instead of warmth, he's just erasing the magnetic strip. *"I just want to get out of here and go home!"* is said over and over until sheer cold, thirst and hunger forces them to return to one of the apartments away from the one with the police car in front. One by one they sneak into a two bedroom apartment. The first on the beds, one in each chair, the rest on the floor. It's better than trying to sleep outside.

The alert policeman keys his mike signaling the next raid. At dawn, they are conveyed to the County Detention Center. A plane lands at BWI Marshall with the next to be detained. He will questioned and tried for murder. For now, Lorenzo, Sis and her brother are safe. But the remaining clone makers are coming...but when?

Angelbots

13

Boomerang

Lorenzo's world seems to have returned to normal. Enough so once more the three friends are studying together. However the angels are becoming increasingly bored with their robotic hosts. Everything's in place to do great things, but no one can think of anything. Then Lorenzo receives a call from the FBI that shakes his world to its' core. The credit card used in an international crime syndicate has been traced back to a company he owns. They want him to come down to their offices to have a talk.

Lorenzo knows better than to go alone. He and his lawyer are ushered into a gray government office. One with the usual desk and two chairs. A big mirror on one wall speaks to the fact their meeting isn't altogether private. The occupant of the desk is a middle aged African American with two sports trophies on a side desk and a note pad in front of him. Matter of factly, he acknowledges to Lorenzo's attorney when asked if the meeting is being recorded

He taps the pad with a pencil looking down, then stares intensely at Lorenzo. *"Your family has a distinguished record of service to the community; how did you become involved with an international crime syndicate?"* Lorenzo's lawyer jumps to his feet shouting, *"What are you implying?"* *"My client hasn't the slightest idea what you are talking about!"* *"Please explain yourself."* The official smiles cordially but continues to look directly at Lorenzo.

"We have someone in custody who has been implicated in biological crimes in several countries." *"He used a credit card issued to a company you own to not only get here but to finance*

twelve terrorists and their weapons, all of which also have in custody." Holding up a booking photo of the missing student from the dead professors' class he asks, *"Do you know this man?"* Lorenzo whispers something to his attorney. *"My client acknowledges having met the individual in the photograph you are holding as a fellow student in a college class."*

"Is this the same class you were taking from an associate of the man we arrested this morning?" Lorenzo is wide eyed with shock and looks at his attorney for guidance. *"This is all a surprise to my client." "May we confer in private."* The official nods yes, *"There is a coffee shop on the first floor, can you be back here in perhaps an hour?"* The attorney agrees and they go to the shop. Lorenzo sputters, *"After my parents suddenly died in that crash I put a team in place to run things until I get my degree." "I can't imagine what's been going on to cause this to happen." "I'm willing to cooperate with the FBI in any way I can but really don't want to go to jail."*

Back in the same office within the hour, the attorney explains Lorenzo's position. The FBI agent, says, *"I need to confer with my supervisor."* He stands and leaves the room. The attorney advises shaking Lorenzo to say nothing until the man returns. They silently wait for what seems forever. The FBI agent returns looking disappointed.

Clearly, he hoped to learn something from their conversation. After listening to the lame conversation they had in the wired coffee shop and the nothingness of conversation they've just had; he believes the boy is innocent. It would be great if he could get him to wear a wire and go into the card issuer's inner sanctum. However, its' obvious to him this kid is too nervous to be undercover. He looks at them. *"I suspect you are telling the truth." "Would you be willing to allow us to put several of our agents into that company with a mission to get to the truth?"* Lorenzo's head bobs up and down *"Yes!"* before his mouth can form the word. The adventure begins.

Lorenzo calls the meeting at his place. Sis, Lou, and their hardware companions arrive with the unseen celestials. They can see he's beside himself with angst when he explains what happened at the FBI. *"Why you?" "What have you got to do with them?"* Sis's eyes are wide with amazement as Lorenzo explains he inherited the company from his parents, who inherited it from hid grandfather. *"I shouldn't have been so trusting." "The only reason I'm trying to get a college degree, besides keeping you two company, is to know enough the run things without having to trust people like this."*

Then he reveals a shocking fact. *"According to the FBI agent, one of our classmates was a really bad guy who was in hiding." "They found him and got him to talk...he was on a mission to kill me!"* Sis screams, *"Oh no!"* Lou's face is ashen, *"If they are going to get to you, they'll have to come through me first!"* The three angels within the robots think the same... *"They will have to come through all of us first."*

At noon, the following day. Lorenzo crosses the road to brief the old Director about the latest events. He reminds Lorenzo that the three robots still have the secret Agency resources he downloaded. *"Call on them if necessary; the physical defenses in case of trouble they can provide are supposedly awesome."* He has no idea of the enormity when the angels are operating them.

Unfortunately for the FBI, their undercover employees are quickly spotted. On the surface, this company manufactures farming equipment based on the needs of third world countries. It does a good

Jack Robertson

job with that worthy effort. But, along the way their Board of Directors has become infested with greedy tyrants who want to control the entire world…thus their desire for clones. To own clones within robots would give them power beyond imagination…

As soon as the Board realizes the FBI is on the property they try to break all links to their clone caper. The remaining scientists have outlived their usefulness and are to be cut loose. In a closed session of the Board with limited invitees, the chairman explains, *"Only their corporate credit cards still link them to us."*

When the cards are cancelled the scientists still need funds from other sources. Even wannabee world dictators must rely on old fashioned financial resources to survive. The ivory tower executives of Lorenzo's rogue management did not inform their accounting group in the closeout of the scientists. It just hung them out to dry and cut off payments and perks. But didn't just forgot to close the cards. No one wanted their name on the order hoping the operation would simply evaporate. As one puts it- *"Business as usual."*

When the three robots error out and shut down, they are sent back to their manufacturers for repairs. At least that is what might

82

seem to be the case if anyone would wonder. In reality, it happens the robot manufacturer is located in the same business park as is the world tool division. Albeit the company officers are unrelated.

As soon as the robots arrive they are uncrated and depart on foot n the direction of their target. They simply adopt the attitude of employees returning to work and flash something perceived by the gate guards to be the proper badges. They walk right in behind arriving employees. It is such an easy strategy just to hide in the open. That's why every spy agency does it. Once past physical security, first they locate the implanted FBI agents but don't make contact. The agents don't realize they've been outed and are working hard.

Lucy, Chippy and Terry, the robotic employees are tastefully dressed. Seemingly ordinary employees, they head for the source of all corporate conversation…the ladies room. They listen, record, and collate all that is spoken. All subjects taboo elsewhere find their way into the inner sanctum of ladies room. They haven't been spotted.

The three Angelbots occupy separate stalls with their panties down at their ankles with appropriate audio. The color of each pair of panties and the shoe color changes very frequently to confuse onlookers. Every conversation is transmitted to the Agency minus ambient background noise.

An undisclosed number of sections within the Agency are devoted to clandestine intelligence analysis No identifiers are needed to donate to its reservoir of information. The Agency knows who is who.

After lunch, a comprehensive report is received with more information than these three need to locate the location of the group who handled the discontinued clone project. Ralph says, *"There's enough scandal to start an armed conflict within this organization."* Rather than create chaos, Lucy, Terry, and Chippy visit their bogus old classmates in the section where the undercover FBI agents are working. The agents welcome the information. However, linking with the outed FBI agents gives company security three more targets…the girls.

Before plant security reacts to the girls, the three siphon the company database of the discontinued clone operation along with everything needed to track their degree of association.] Including names, addresses, associates. Its' encoded murderous history is transmitted to the Agency. Lucien informs her cohorts, *"A raid is scheduled for four o'clock."*

By 3.00 p.m. the trio have signed out at the guard post and are on their way back to their manufacturer. There they are immediately approved for return to Maryland. Fellow angel, Roman lightheartedly labels Ralph *"a hacker,"* Ralph agrees, but insists he is a *white hat hacker*. Roman laughs, *"Whatever, the hell that means!"*

Roman has been an angel for eons, so Ralph simply holds his tongue rather than stir up old jealous feelings. Fortunately, Ralph's hacking worked so well the factory didn't attempt to disassemble the robots. Who knows what would have happened? Instead, they are put onboard Lorenzo's foundation jet and seated in a comfortable part of the plane with a card table. Their choice, monopoly leaves the angelbots in a bitter struggle for Park Place and Boardwalk. By the time they get to Lorenzo's. Chippy actually must be plugged in to recharge. Monopoly is more stressful than the operation. Angels vs. Robots is brutal.

Except for when they play games with the angels, the robots are put into standby mode. Otherwise, the robots and the angels would compete to dominate conversations and actions. An unintentional byproduct is the robots are gradually assuming the angel's personalities. Their control, of the mechanical girls is nearly over. Angel, Ralph was a vigilante in a t past reality. This was obliterated when he married Lucien. His transferred personality doesn't have a quiet angelic nature, just the opposite.

Chippy, who Ralph took on this mission just isn't about to go back to being just a toy. These angels have a new dynamic method of recharging. It will extend their range exponentially. All retain the ability to tap into the ambient power grid. And will just top off their batteries when plugged in to recharge. Their artificial intelligence, personality infusion, and unlimited power combined with their clandestine experience render them nearly invincible.

No other 9000 teaching aids are even close. A fundamental flaw: they lack the biological advantage of cellular growth. Machines wear out. As the world invents robots with biological regeneration these 9000 s will seem primitive.

Hawk flies in with a message from the heavens. *"Your mission as Angelbots is finished."* *"The clone headquarters is closed and no link to the illicit clone factory is operational." "The pursuit of the remaining scientists who were a part of that murder and clone business is also being handled." "You three are back on double duty as guardian angels." "There still aren't enough of us to simply devote to one human being." "Others have been covering for you." "Your mission is a success." "By the way, you are asked to avoid the board game Monopoly in the future." "Your intensely competitive natures while playing nearly set the earths' atmosphere ablaze."* Having delivered his message, Hawk flies off without another word trying to appear as if he's on another important mission. Once out of the angels view, he meets up with Dumas. They're going hunting for skunk…or muskrat.

The human trio is sitting in the living room playing games other than Monopoly. They're becoming bored with their robots. It's the way of intelligent creatures. On the other hand, Sis and Lorenzo seem increasingly interested in one another. Neither gives a second thought to Lou. As Sis always says, *"Lou is just Lou, he's my brother and I love him but he's a bit dull."*

Soon Dumas and Hawk return looking sheepish, the angels float off leaving Dumas in charge. Hawk doesn't go inside. And Dumas obviously can't fly. The plan they are to follow in case of a threat is for Dumas to alert Hawk. Then Hawk will alert the angels. For now there's no apparent threat to the three friends.

The robots are growing more restless than even the angels and are no longer inactive when left alone. Chippy gets the others to sneak out back from time to time. She whips out her laser wand and knocks down a low hanging branch. The others follow her example and within minutes the backyard looks as if a storm blew through. Terrified, by the chaos the owl flutters and flies away. Turning down the beam strength to illuminate only they pass the time chasing, hiding, and illuminating one another. Now it's time to go in and resume waiting for something to happen. Sis and Lou take them home, but they aren't the placid robots who started the day. Their circuits are hot and restless; these girls are looking for action. The games are over, Sis and Lou take them home. They will look for every opportunity to exist up to their potential.

Angelbots

14

Awakening

"Now it's as if I'm Ralph an avenging angel instead of a mechanical being." Chippy explains to Terry and Lucy her robot associates how something strange transformed her into something else last night. *"One minute I was standing on my recharging station without a care when I heard someone cry out for help."* *"Without a program, or instruction to guide me my legs took me to a fast food store."* *" There a clerk was screaming for help from inside of a freezer."* *"A robber locked her in after emptying the cash register."*

"As soon as I got her out she alerted police." "I didn't wait around to answer questions."

As much as they each wanted their own robot toy, Sis Lou and Lorenzo become bored with these. In their original configuration these teaching aids would be content to sit on a shelf. The uploads from the old Agency Director, that Terry shared, and the angel bot adventure have left these with an almost human energy. They know their potential and Chippy's rescue of the clerk ignites a spark of independence within all three. As one puts it, *"I want to kick tail and take names!"* Lucy gives her a stern rebuke saying, *"You mean Serve and Protect."*

After Sis's basketball coach calls her out for using a ringer to practice, robots are permanently benched. The three humans are excellent students and need little academic help. So, there is nothing for the 9000 s to do except sit on their chargers and wait. They communicate with one another from separate locations through the Agency link. It wasn't turned off.

The Agency always has someone looking to exploit a possible resource. Three seemingly human robots have too much potential.

And there are abundant anomalies to clear for the safety of the public. Robert, a young new analyst is assigned to keep and eye on them to maintain and report anything of interest. Although Robert is quiet he's just as ambitious as the three stuck on their chargers.

Weeks go by, then a month, their conversations are becoming increasingly restless. Robert makes an unauthorized move. He hopes to assist and monitor them, so he introduces himself. Speaking on their channel. *"My name is Robert." "I'm with the Agency and I'm here to help you." "I would like to help you fulfill your desires."* An offer like this is exactly what they are waiting for. Even intelligent machines need goals. They need a Robert to give them purpose.

He begins to develop goals by listening to others at the Agency discuss their budgetary and resource limitations. Starting small, he focuses upon an unsolved theft from the Agency. Then feeds the problem to the mechanical trio. They analyze cam records in the area for some indication of the items' location. Within hours it's spotted in a pawnshop very close to the Agency owned by an ostensibly foreign national. The local police monitor pawnshop records for stolen goods. Robert quickly enters the missing laptop into their list. The owner is visited, and the laptop is confiscated. The laptop is delivered to the main gate guard post with a courtesy note by a County policeman. The police ask no questions because from experience they know not to ask questions of Agency staff. Everyone involved just exchanges a mutually understood wide eyed smile.

Without disclosing details, Robert picks up the laptop and returns it to inventory saying to the clerk, *"This was returned to us by the Anne Arundel County Police Department." "They were informed of its' location by an anonymous source."* Having cleared that obstacle, he tracks down the contractor who pilfered the article in the first place.

He calls her speaking in a low intimate tone, *"We know what you did, and we are watching you."* He makes it a point to pass by where she is working to see the expression on her face but doesn't speak. Her face is gray with fear, and her body quakes as though cold. She has no idea who is watching her. For next to nothing pawn shop cash she will look over her shoulder for the rest of her life. Her dishonesty has left her helpless. Wherever she goes she imagines eyes are following. She is as submissive as the robots. The creepy voice now owns her.

Young Robert has another resource, one only he knows…a thief. Well, actually not just him; he left his channel open. His robotic girls know too. He knows how much they want to be active. The thief can't know who he is, but he wants the three robots to know him as a friend. One they can rely upon to respect them as more than just machines. Because unlike their owners, he knows they can have desires.

This people he works with still have not come to see him as the developed agent. These assets will let them know he has arrived. If he does something significant with them his accomplishments will be appreciated. For now he only reports their communications with one another minus any reference to his with them. And nothing about the terrified thief. *Need to know* works both ways.

"I want the name of everyone you know is stealing." When she receives this demand, the thief feels she has a way to exonerate herself by proving her loyalty. She starts with the one who she got the idea from, her best friend.

But when she tries to start up a conversation on the subject with the friend, she's cut short. Word has gotten around the crooked pawnshop owner has closed shop. There isn't another with such a dishonest operation within miles. It's too dangerous to steal now, or even talk. Anyone might be wearing a wire. When her friend sees the tears in her eyes she quickly adds, *"Of course I trust you…"*

When she reports back after Robert calls he assures her not to worry and to keep her eyes open for something to report the next time he calls. She can tell from the ring tone that he is in the building. There is no caller ID. The internal security people suspect something's wrong and report it up the chain of command. But no one knows. The top cop in security knows everything. The pawn shop sting was his idea. The new place is located near another government facility. He knows someone in the Agency ruined his sting. Because he's so new, no one suspects young Robert would even go to lunch without saying *"May I?"*

Thrilled with his success so far, Robert invites the clones to meet him, one at a time, at a sandwich shop where college students and t tutors regularly meet. So many students and tutors are gathered at tables in pairs this couple will completely blend in.

Lorenzo doesn't know she's gone. Because he hasn't opened the room where she's supposed to be in days. Chippy navigated here on her first bus ride. Sensing the need for a charge, she taps the ambient electric field by herself for the first time. It makes her feel alive.

Arriving, Chippy is somewhat confused at first. A number of people look up and smile. Robert approaches her table. Extending his hand, *"Chippy, I'm Robert, your tutor."* The place is crowded but their table sits in a corner. He asks, *"What will you have?"* Then he remembers she doesn't eat and says, *"I haven't eaten; I'll be right back."* She slyly looks around and sees only anxious students. One older man nearby is receiving instructions about his statistics course. He is in over his head. The teaching aid in her causes her to whisper several words to them that seems to clarify the solution to a hypothesis problem. The student gets it and gives her his apple. The tutor just shakes his head at the intrusion.

When the student goes to get him more coffee, the tutor whispers with a strained smile, *"Find your own dummy!"* Fortunately, Robert returns and has his own apple. She tucks hers into her pocket and will take it back to the house for Dumas. They talk about the weather. He asks her to scan the room for possible foreign agents from a list he holds in front of her. There are only students and tutors.

Robert complements her; she gives him her programed, *you're trying to give me a snowjob* look but says nothing. She suggests his lunchtime is over and he get back the work. They leave.

Robert has met his match and wonders if lunches with his remaining two it will go any easier. She gets back to the house just early enough to miss going in with Lorenzo. The apple is still in her pocket. Lorenzo opens her storage room where she now stands dutifully at her charging station. His eyes bug out when he sees the apply protruding from her pocket. Lorenzo is so surprised he blurts out, *"Chippy!"* She smile innocently and hands him her apple. *"Where did the apple come from?"* Chippy makes sounds a robot is supposed to make and recites, *"Apple tree in Washington State."* Lorenzo realizes that's all she's going to say.

He accepts it. *"Thank you!"* Charmingly Chippy smiles saying, *"You are welcome Renzo."* Then she rolls back her eyes bleating, *"Chippy needs to be recharged."* Lorenzo forgets to ask where she got the idea he was just to be called *"Renzo."* He just takes a bite and stomps out saying, *"Renzo needs a charge too!"* Chippy yells back sarcastically, *"Go find Sis and maybe both of you can recharge!"* Chippy answers, *"That woman loves you!"* Dumas just burps and wishes he got the apple instead.

Robert repeats his interviews with the other two and comes away suspecting that instead of acquiring three assets he has been acquired. Without remembering he's bugged. Although he can hear them; they can hear him. And they are learning fast. He wonders why he now hears echoes on their channel. Ordinarily an analyst could call a technician. He can't without tipping off his superiors at the Agency.

The three robots sense others within the supposedly secure facility are also bugged intermittently. Some are even on their frequency. The mixture of downloads they've received have infused a sense of loyalty to the Agency. They will trace the transmissions with or without poor Robert. But how?

As Robert moves around with his com open they record the signal strength of each conversation. When it's heard again they compare to determine who is talking and about what. An individual might have a difficult time collating these bits and pieces of information. These girls do not because within the downloaded programs is the training package for analysts. They are the newest unsung Agency analysts.

The three girls divide the task and soon have an audio diagram of everything Robert passes everywhere he walks. Surprisingly, nothing intelligent is copied from men's room conversations because there are none…just splashing and flushing.

On several occasions they hear both sides of a conversation. Within a week they know the names and duties of the bugged employees. However they can't know who might be listening to Robert and themselves. So, when they communicate, they turn off their internal links to the Agency. They know how to adjust themselves to their various modes.

They design a code and will follow a daily revision similar to the World War II enigma system. Hopefully, they can trace those who are spying on them. Their side talk is such that they don't use their assigned frequency.

After these conferences with Robert they will know who is copying their transmission the second time suggested by comparing who was present the first time. It's a very simple process of elimination. Robert still isn't willing to involve the Agency's modern techniques until they detect a real threat.

Within a day of deciphering their high speed code, Robert realizes he has to catch up with them or be left behind. He tells them he wants to get together at the same place for another meeting.

Knowing the buggers are listening and were unseen at each of the initial meetings, he also feels the same people will be there again. This time he won't restrict the girls to a list. These spies aren't on his list. They have a good amount of data to analyze. Robotic memory includes everything, conversations, and digital clips of even the cars on the parking lot. Plus everyone on the buses on the way to and from the meetings.

Jack Robertson

Arriving at the meeting place they find mostly the same faces as the first time. Tutors and students are conducting business as before. It will take more analysis back at Robert's duty section along with some Agency tools available only on site to separate the real tutors from the rats.

At their homes, the girls decide another way to mix things up is to use old copper landlines. Because metal wire is so easily tapped, they plan to reduce that risk by again using the code of the day in each communication. Anyone listening might assume they are listening to an old fax.

It's unnecessary; these particular rats would never imagine such a high tech operation still uses copper wire landlines. Instead, they triangulate the positions of each robot using their routine daily transmissions.

What's more, the rats clearly understand why their own Agency bugs have echoes. Now they are on their way to eliminate these strange women who are hindering their spying on their own Agency spies.

The rats cars discretely park several doors away from the center of triangulation. Hopes to capture Lucy, Chippy or Terry fail because repeaters, transmitters that only relay signals, have been disbursed to confuse. But the buggers have figured out the robots are in the same places as Sis, Lou, and Lorenzo.

It's an unlucky coincidence. Today the girls are stuck at their charging stations to maintain secrecy from their human possessors. This is rare for the three humans almost never change their routine. Only one person notices the buggers. The retired Agency Director across from Lorenzo's house immediately catches on and alerts his permanent security detail. The buggers operate in shifts rotating cars to the three subjects. The security detail alerts Homeland, and the detail realizes three are surveilled by an adverse power.

The Director is astounded by his neighbors blindness to the surveillance. It's time to call Lorenzo over for tea. *"Lorenzo, my friend, could you please stop by after dinner to help us move some things?"* Lorenzo immediately recalls from past experience something is amiss.

Dumas yawns and heads out of the pantry dog door. He looks up but the Hawk isn't on the chimney. He feels Hawk should know what's going on and lets out an eerie low howl that alerts every angel in the valley. By the time Lorenzo reaches the Directors' front door, Hawk has reported to the angels and the angels are in the room with their human charges. Then the three robots spontaneously upload everything to the angels...including their relationship with the hapless Agency analyst.

This afternoon Robert is watching the Baltimore Orioles play the New York Yankees. It's tied going into the ninth when his ears start ringing and his eyes water. A little twinge goes off in his conscience telling him to immediately inform his Agency superior of his activities. The Orioles lose.

And he's doubting he's going to win after confessing how far his rogue operation has advanced beyond their instruction to observe and report. To himself, *"You are in a world of trouble!" "Thank God no one's dead."* Three others are thinking along the same lines but at least they can blame it on the government. Robert hasn't thought of this aspect yet, but he will. The Government is the invisible victim of everyone's blame.

Angelbots

15

Resolution

Robert's section leader looking half asleep and somewhat drawn meets him just inside of the secure area. *"This better be good!"* *"I was up half the night with a sick kid and was just falling asleep."* Robert sheepishly acknowledges, *"It's not great!"* Looking up at a camera, *"Extremely the opposite."*

Intuitively the leader also glance up at the overhead camera and guides him down a corridor into a secure room. The walls are padded to deaden sound. White sound is all around them to block every sound from getting through any cracks. And the ever present cameras are absent. Some information is so sensitive the Agency must hide it from others within these walls.

His superior's eyes gloss over as Robert explains the full scope of his actions. The man nods in approval of the laptop retrieval and smiles thinly at turning its' thief into an asset. Robert is slightly encouraged until he drops the robot bombshell.

"Robert, all you were supposed to do was facilitate and monitor their communications." "Who in hell told you to play double Oh Seven man?" "What you've got going is way beyond my pay grade!" "Go home, get some sleep; I'll let you know after I report and am told what to do." His section head leaves to make his report. On his way out Robert passes the gate guards without even looking at them.

He drives home at the precise posted speed limit with his stomach in knots, cold sweat running down the back of his neck.

Tower security is suspicious of cars doing the precise speed limit on nearly empty highways in the Agency area and run his plates and are satisfied. Once his head hits the pillow oddly though, he immediately falls asleep. In his mind, he sleeps the slumber of one who is condemned.

It isn't long before he realizes his phone is beeping. It's that urgent beep reserved for work. The voice simply orders, *"Please report to the Director's office as soon as possible."*

Taking only enough time to shower, shave and put on clean underwear and shirt. Wearing the same suit and tie, Robert runs out of the door and slams his car into drive. He heads back into the dawn at exactly five over the limit, an excess tolerated in the State.

The guards scan his ID without visible emotion. As he races up to the elevator they says to one another in unison, *"The world is coming to an end, women and children into the lifeboats first!"* Joking is their only way of dealing with the stress of knowing they work in the world's premier information gathering site without the slightest idea what's happening until it's on the news.

Arriving at the Director's suite he's guided to a conference room. The Director greets him with surprisingly cordial sarcasm. *"I wish I had the ability to just do whatever makes sense to me; the way you do!"* *"I just don't have that luxury."*

There's a knock at the conference room door. An army major peeks in, *"Should I send them up now?"* The Director nods affirmatively. The door swings completely open. In walk, three smiling robots, three humans, and three who no one here can see. Plus one retired Agency Director. Then an orderly brings in coffee and donuts. The Director welcomes them saying *"Please help yourself."* Only the haggard section leader budges.

"I have asked my predecessor to join us this morning because several of you have met him before." *"And, he has assured me that you are fine and loyal young adults."* Smiles all around with sidelong glances at the old Director. *"Starting immediately, I want to personally ask each of you to be extremely careful."* *"You have somehow become involved with what appears to be an international espionage activity that we are just beginning to understand."* In truth, no one in the Agency knows how deep the espionage goes. *"I also*

understand the three of you known as the 9000 series teaching aids have been modified to a point far beyond anything we can imagine." *"I would like to ask you to decide now if you are with us or wish to be allowed to return to a more dormant state?"* *"We recognize that you now have all of the emotions of humans, without the benefits."* Chippy raises a very human looking hand. The Director nods to her saying, *"Please speak."* The three angels are not in possession of the robots now and also await her answer.

Chippy without hesitation informs the group that she and her two associates agree their purpose is to serve humankind. *"We feel the best way to do so is to maintain our considerably modified state, rather than going back to factory settings."* The Director asks, *"Do you have anything to add to what we already know?"* Three robots simultaneously exhibit an emotion never entered within their programs, a mischievous grin. *"Yes, we do!"* *"As we were entered your building, we coordinated the information we have collected recently with the diagram of this building."* *"If you promise not to hurt any of your employees we expose as innocent transmitters of sound on the frequency on which we communicate, we are willing to walk you through this facility and others identifying those innocent people."*

"Furthermore, we have reason to believe the human possessors of our physical system are in imminent danger because their homes are under constant surveillance." The old Director nods saying, *"Not as much as you think, at least for now because we have identified and are holding their outer circle." "Through my own security detail, we identified and have apprehended several of them."*

"They are being questioned in accord with current standards of interrogation even now." "I also have enlisted outside contractors with special training to be certain no stone unturned in this search for answers." The present Agency Director, says to his aid, *"Please have a security detail accompany Ms. Chippy and her two associates around these facilities to discover any problems." "Assign a more secure frequency to these fine people?"*

"Robert, you are now in charge of a special project involving Lorenzo, Sis and Lou." "You are to meet with Security immediately." "They are expecting you." "Take Sis, Lou and Lorenzo with you, if

that's OK with the three of you?" Lou answers for them, *"Hell yeah man!"* Three stunned friends follow trying to sort out in their own minds how this all happened when they weren't paying attention to their toys. Sis grabs a box full of donuts on the way out for later.

The new Director invites the old one to lunch; he accepts. After everyone passes through the guard post with relaxed expressions the stern faced guards turn to one another. One jokes, *"Toot toot, this was only a lifeboat drill."* Cupping his hands like a megaphone, *"Everyone stand down and return to your quarters."* Then the other, *"Just another day at the funny farm!"* The other warns, *"Here comes someone, suck it in!"*

Back at his home, Lorenzo welcomes his new live in guests. Lou, Sis, and their mother will have a second home with him. To confuse anyone watching, they will vary where they stay without a pattern. He has enough empty rooms, so they have no problem finding one. Chippy still has her own as well, At Lou and Sis's it's an entirely different matter. To begin with, Mom can't be told anything. They think she'd tell everyone in the neighborhood, at church and on social media.

They lie. They tell her the four big guys occupying Sis and Lou's room are in their class in school and they have lost their lease because the hunting equipment they have. *"No mom, they're very tidy, stay out of their way."* *"They need their privacy!"* *"No ma, they don't drink beer in their rooms, it's against their religion."* Mom pretends she believes what she knows is nonsense. She knows the difference between hunting rifles and military assault weapons. Their new secondary home says even more. Even with all of the unusual changes, Mom pretends not to be curious. When she's alone she practices her own defense drills and no one's the wiser.

When Sis tells Lorenzo how big and strong they are, he finds himself feeling jealous for the first time. Sis watches him turn red croaking, *"You tell me if any of those jackasses do anything!"* She's pleasantly indignant that he would think any of our nation's finest Marines would have anything but perfect manners. Lou stokes it remembering the bait fish Renzo put in his sandwich that day on the boat. *"Renzo, if you think you can take on one of those muscle men, you better start working out!"* Lorenzo doesn't say anything and clams up.

In the morning, when he hears his four Marine guards doing their warmups, he asks if he can join them. Considering his dog is giving them the furry eyeball, they go along with his request. Then Dumas tries to work out too and the whole event becomes hilarious. One asks, *"Is that damn bird up there laughing at us?"* He points his finger up at the chimney pretending to shoot Hawk. The raven squawks something that sounds for all the world like, *"Make my day fool!"* And when everyone stops to look at Hawk, he just flies over to the other side of the roof where no one can see him. Dumas smirks, *"Who's the dumbass now?"*

The FBI is called in when one of the Agency facilities is stalked by an individual taking photos of personnel. These naive government workers walk around with their badges out when they arrive at a nearby shopping center for lunch. The individual has his camera confiscated but he is found to have diplomatic immunity, practically proving his malice. The camera is returned with a completely blank sim card. The old one with the photos is used to print out photos for the naïve classified employees to think about when their performance reviews bear negative comments.

The fall guy for Robert's unauthorized escapade, the new Director is asked to step down over the incident. When asked to name his temporary replacement, he nominates the Old Director. He in turn agrees to serve only until a suitable party can be picked. After Robert's replacement scans the intercepted conversations, it's determined the incident was a plot by a foreign interest to dethrone the fired director as he was too effective in hiding information they wanted. Of course, that's what he was supposed to do, but it made him a target.

As a face saving device, the tarnished one is sent to Washington to serve as liaison to Congress. Rather than a reprimand, Robert is bumped up a pay grade and now is on an equal footing with his former superior. Who now feels overlooked and underappreciated…and is.

Robert puts a good word in for him and he catches up with his colleagues. The Agency finally realizes his value and is providing him a nanny for his children. Something exceeding rare the sacked Director can pull off because he's on his way out of the Agency. The new/old Director says he has plausible deniability because he wasn't sworn in yet when it happened.

When the foreign power who unseated the Director turns out to be a staunch ally, the blame is allowed to fall upon a far less friendly foreign power. They deny the whole affair but by now everyone thinks they were the ones who dethroned the Director after all. They're happy with the misconception because it makes them seem more powerful than they really are. Sis, Lou, and Lorenzo take their toys much more seriously.

The new temporary Director is happy to stick it to the wrongly blamed power because. *"After all they're the assholes who surveilled me sitting on the commode all that time."* He's extremely self-conscious walking around the building realizing some of those with tears in their eyes means they are remembering the dimple on his booty cheeks.

At first he tries to be a good sport. Whenever some fool lets him know his bum has been on display he covers his embarrassment by doing a little dance and shaking it in their face. After a month or so the whole thing is forgotten, except for employees who were on vacation when he returned.

When the old guy has had enough bum humor, he has Robert put out the word that anyone who does anything to disparage his backside is on midnight shift forever. Someone in IT dares; and is found out. After remarking the Director is a bootyful guy a bit too loud as he walks by, she finds herself driving home after working all night blinking like an owl at the morning sun. Thinking... *"It wasn't that good."*

After more successful triangulation, the headquarters of the insurgent operation spawned by the clone operation is pinpointed and closed down with several dozen arrests including their thugs

The internal spying operation is an entirely different problem. Their entire group are herded onto an unmarked cargo plane. They are warned if they ever are caught again they will be thrown out over the ocean using rotten moth eaten parachutes. Neither side believes this and both the captors and the spies chuckle.

Outed spies are traded for one another by most governments. A trade for a lone American businessman captured and wrongly accused of espionage by the incorrectly accused enemy power is enacted. Both sides leak the spies were actually double agents to chill any further covert activities. And some countries take these allegations so seriously they chemically induce mind altering drugs to their own agents. But not the United States.

The foreign plot is blown; hopefully, there's no need for concern Sis, Lou or Lorenzo will be harmed. Both embassies, the one taking the blame, recall their ambassadors. The new liaison to Congress reports back to the Agency, *"Trade isn't affected, but the State Department has put out a travel advisory."*

Only half of the Marines are still at each home of the human trio. All three of the teenager's bodies have become buff from working out. Mom secretly has been doing the same. Lorenzo and Sis cheat on the diet and are sneaking out for milkshakes regularly. They burn up the extra calories without picking up weight. Lou feels like he's missing out on what his sister and best friend have and is looking for someone too.

His new Marine buddies convince him to accompany them to a night spot in a nearby Wallow City. After several beers, Lou decides to join the Marines. On hearing his news, his mother tells her remaining two Marine guards to locate to new digs. Permission is granted to them to return to the barracks. Lou drops out of college with the idea of becoming Marine. Sis and Lorenzo are proud, even if Mom isn't happy.

A hit man waits in the cold in a just down the street from Sis, Lou, and Mom. He hasn't heard from the party who hired him, but he hopes to conclude his part of the deal, collect the balance and head for somewhere warm. His knuckles clench and open around a cold hard object in his pocket. He has been waiting like this every Thursday for the last two weeks. Tomorrow is the day the trash is collected in this neighborhood.

The departure of the last two Marines was premature.

The thug is about to call it a night when a figure appears at the door of the house in question. Stealthily, he slips out of the car leaving the door slightly ajar. No sign of alarm is apparent. The thug knows better than to make a sound. He regards himself a professional. Just as Lou reaches the curb, a steel object comes out of nowhere and crushes his skull. He is maneuvered into a large bag and dragged down to a house with a *"Sold"* sign. No one has occupied the home since the last resident left. When trash is collected around dawn, this parcel will be picked up along with everything else. Mom and Sis have gone to bed. His security detail is readjusting to barracks life and will never again taste Moms' home cooking.

A bespectacled gentleman walks his wife's big Standard Poodle down the pavement towards the trash with contents containing Lou's rigid body. The black dog controls where they go. The man holding his leash is simply pulled from side to side as it sniffs and raises a hind leg at each place along the long pavement.

The one holding the leash is half asleep. Reaching Lou's garbage bag, rather than raise his hind leg to mark territory, he sniffs and claws the green plastic bag with a paw repeatedly breaking through the seal. A whoosh of air breaks through. The poodle scratches excitedly at the bundle awaking the man holding his leash. Alert to what appears to be the dog digging into someones leftover dinner, he drags his whining poodle forcefully down the street. Overpowered and helpless to communicate the dog obediently resumes his walk and soon forgets the reason for his irritation. Poodles look smarter than they are. Some people are also the same.

Several streets away the clang and bang of the garbage truck is heard as it comes nearer. Lou's garbage bag is hefted by strong hands into the stinking yawning throat of the truck and is soon covered by loose and bagged refuse. The night gives way to dawn and neither Sis nor Mom know poor Lou is gone. He's literally down in the dumps.

The bags were not crushed because the carrier was so full. And poor Lou's isn't dead. The truck is full and returns to its' gate at the landfill. It is the last in line and Lou within his garbage bag are beneath the pile. The trucks dump their loads, so lucky Louis is on top. So, in the end, as it is said, the first shall be last; the last shall be first. Maybe this is what that all is about. The winter sun shines brightly warming his bag. Seagulls circle like vultures. One spies the hole in Lou's bag.

Mom is in the kitchen; Sis sits up in bed. After a while they will miss one's son, the others' brother. Mom's first alarm is when she looks in his room and sees bis bed. *"Sis,"* she yells, it hasn't been slept in. Sis, replies and suggests *"Maybe, he's over at Renzo's"* But in her heart she knows that it just isn't so. And she calls to no avail. Lorenzo hasn't seen him either. She brings up his robot. Obviously, she hasn't, for no one saw the contractor out front make his move. Lou won't be coming home for a while.

High above the landfill the black raven hovers. For a strange sight has his attention. With a sea of leftovers so enticing, the seagulls and sparrows peck at only one. A big green bag with the body and soul of poor Lou is their quest. Hawk gives a mighty call. And angels surround the poor lad at the center of it all. Sore Lou moves out of the bag and the gulls retreat. But still there is too much pain in his head to get to his feet. Hawk dives down and picks the bag away and Lou comes to his wits.

But his rescue isn't complete. He has amnesia and terrible pain in his head. He looks at Hawk and asks, *"Am I alive or am I dead?"* Hawk can only nod to the angels. But Lou doesn't see anyone but the raven. He's alive but can't remember his name.

A landfill volunteer, out on work detail from a place of detention thinks Lou is a landfill scavenger, looking for something to take, warns, *"You better beat feet before the man catches you!"* Lou staggers out of the heap and up the hill to somewhere. It isn't clear where, as long as it's not down there. Hawk leaves Lou in the care of angels. They can see him although Lou can't see them. A strong blast of wind pumps oxygen into Lou and blows the seagulls away.

Flying as fast as he can, Hawk lands on his chimney and calls out for old Dumas. The dog alerts Chippy, who runs to Lorenzo. *"I have calculated the location of Louis, your missing classmate."* *"He is in serious trouble and needs you to help him."*

Lorenzo calls Sis from the car as he follows Chippy's directions. She in turn is watching Hawk high above. Sis tells her mother. Her mother screams, *"What happened to him?"* But no one can say. Staggering and falling on the road from the landfill, everyone just sees only a drunk. Then Lorenzo's car comes into sight.

Lou's panic subsides when Lorenzo pulls up beside him as says soothingly, *"Are you alright buddy?"* Lou mumbles, *"Don't know; do I know you?"* Lorenzo is too choked up to speak. Chippy answers for him, *"Louis, he's your best friend; please get into the car." "Ok, but I don't remember anything."* The car stops. Lorenzo helps him into the back seat and tells Chippy to sit in back.

As the car takes off Chippy sees the injury to Lou's head. The bleeding has stopped. Blood forms a solid dry clot beyond his ears. Chippy and her associates have only a minor cache of medical knowledge and voice response. Although Lorenzo was heading towards Lou's home, Chippy states firmly, *"This student has serious head injuries and must be transported to a trauma center."* She then dials 911 and Lorenzo coordinates his course with the point an ambulance will intercept. Then he calls Lou's mother to tell her. At once Mom is relieved and then in panic. *"Sis, your brother is alive, but Lorenzo is taking him to the hospital." "He's been hurt!"* Sis screams and they get dressed. Then they sit and wait for a call because they don't know which hospital. Lorenzo sits in the trauma center waiting room and doesn't call because he hasn't been told anything. Chippy sits calmly in download watching the hospital angels hover overhead.

The murderous contractor also waits and is watching for the rest of his blood money. It isn't in the account. He's amazed, *"This isn't ever supposed to happen!"* But it happened because those who hired him aren't around. He has enough money to get to somewhere warm but not enough to live the good life. As far as finding work, forget it. They have a whole lot more of his kind than there are around here. Once there…nothing to do.

Angelbots

16

Mobilization

Months go by without a normal happy Lou in the lives of Sis, Mom and Lorenzo. Lou gradually becomes himself again after leaving the hospital and spending countless hours in rehabilitation. The doctors tell the family his physical recovery is going exceptionally well due to his fine physical condition at the time of *the accident. "Accident?" "Bullfeathers!"*

Sis and Mom go from neighbor to neighbor asking whether anyone saw Lou being mugged. Finally, one neighbor across from them realizes she has the entire event recorded on her laptop from an outside camera. The figures are blurry, but the tag number is very clear. Police track the tag to a rental car company. And then to a fictitious name and address. The contractor ditched the insurance card at the moment he got back to his room. Fortunately, the picture on his phony drivers license is real. So they know what he looks like.

Terry, Lou's usual robot, was slow to pick up the chase because Mom and Sis were so busy visiting Lou in the hospital they didn't think of her as a tool. Finally Terry communicates the problem to Chippy through Robert at the Agency. Facial recognition has a problem identifying him. The process stalls for almost two weeks, then a hit. Several hits in fact. The photo appears on several passports and two drivers license photos including the one he used to rent the car used in the hit. But where is he now? In fact he's walking down the same street in front of where Lou was taken after his so-called accident…Shock Trauma in Baltimore.

It doesn't help Mom to realize the thug who almost took Lou's life is still out there ready to strike at either of her children. She doesn't know what else to do after asking the police to pay special attention to her home. The angels know everything about the contractor. Again, they can't directly intervene. Once again they download themselves into the robots. Hawk tells Dumas *"The contractor's in for a world of hurt!"* The owl in the tree just says… *"Who?"*

The thug continues to wait in vain for the balance of his fee for disposing Lou. Waiting around is boring. So he hangs out at bars in the city hoping to find someone to con out of money, or maybe to roll. To his wonder and joy a pair of twins seem taken by him. He repeatedly orders them drinks thinking they'll be easier to take advantage of once drunk.

It seems to work; they begin slurring their words and head for the ladies room to *"powder their noses"* when in reality it's to empty the liquid their pocketbooks. Seeming to barely make it back to their tables, they suggest to him they'd like to see his place. *"I can't believe my luck!"*

The delusional hit man shows them around his rented room at the hotel then the three settle back on the couch to get cozy. Minutes later he starts feeling sleepy. As he blanks out he realizes in shock, *"I'm their mark!"* He drools as his lights go out, *"Be nice ladies."*

Some time later, he comes to. It's down in the dank cold basement of the building. He isn't wearing a stitch of clothes and something else is missing. Touching himself where it hurts the most, he realizes two of his most prized parts have been removed; he is now a gelding. Survival is foremost on his mind as he grabs a dirty towel from the laundry and fashions himself a covering for his disgraced area.

He knows he's still in his hotel by markings on the wall. The injured thug limps painfully to the end of the hall. An elevator door slides open when he presses a silver button. Once inside, he pushes the number for his floor. It continues past disregarding his request until it reaches the roof. There, it stops; the doors slide open to a brisk blowing winter snow.

He gets off to get on another that works, one that will stop at his floor. It doesn't. Furiously he pushes buttons until his fingers are numb. Too dead to feel anything. Pushing his hands into his armpits warms them slightly. Then he realizes there is only one place on body warmer. It helps; it hurts.

As he stands shivering two more elevators open. Unwilling to return to the useless lift that got him to the top, he limps into the shelter of one. Obviously, he can't get into his room without the key. So, still keeping his numb fingers in the warmest place of his body, the contractor uses his knee to press the lobby button. *"Nobody will be there this late,"* he hopes. The elevator doors to the lobby slide wide exposing him to an enormous party in progress including an open bar where everyone starts clapping.

Except for the drunks on bar stools, those partying pay almost no attention to the naked man. One who stands with his freeing thumbs jammed up his backside to prevent frostbite. He rushes over to the desk and begs for his room key. The clerk sees his condition and turns red. *"Sir, I am so sorry to tell you this, but you are checked out."* *"During the restoration of your room our people found the items in this envelope."* The clerk hands him the large envelope from behind the counter. The stunned contractor hasn't a free hand to take it. So the clerk obligingly tucks it under his chin. Now he can't speak for fear of dropping the heavy package. *"Sir, I am willing to call you a cab."* Contractor wags his head *"No."* He just keeps glaring at the clerk, gritting his teeth and loudly grunting.

The clerk reaches his limit of being threatened. Hotel security arrives and ushers him through the applauding crowd to the front door. Snow still swirls down once through the brass doors. Rather than risk a lawsuit by tossing his naked body onto the slippery sidewalk they call the police. He has a death grip with his chin on the package hopefully containing his overdue fee. Frozen fingers too numb to retrieve from his bum, he struggles against leaving the doors.

Baltimore's finest arrive. He is pushed by hotel security and pulled by the police. They threaten to use their taser gun. He leaps into the paddy wagon. He's had enough.

As the door is slammed shut, the body heat generated by the struggle has warmed him enough to partly melt his fingers, but not quite enough. As he squats trying not to be cooperative, the object he used to hit poor Lou falls out onto the ground. One police officer handcuffs him; the other retrieves the metal object. *"You won't be needing this for some time!"*

Although his hands still aren't free to grasp his paper package yet, the police realize he needs medical treatment. They take him to a facility where once the handcuffs are removed he gets to open his envelope. Inside, he finds his wallet and a receipt for the accumulated room and added services. A lot of added drinks...

The unlimited open bar receipt for all of the guests of the party is included. They applauded him as he left for his generosity in paying for their open bar. As the paddy wagon pulled away he recalls their happy voices in the winter night. He is broke and the *limit exceeded* state of his credit card tells him he needs to seek refuge in a hospital or jail. And the twins have competed the work of the angels.

The man can see what the two lumps are in the plastic inner bag of the envelope. They're jewels he wouldn't have willingly given up. At least he can look at them in a jar he can carry wherever he goes, whenever he is released. They judge orders psychiatric evaluation.

And has justice truly been served? *"Not by a long shot!,"* according to the angel Roman. *"Lou doesn't know his attacker is in the booby hatch and wouldn't think he received justice if he knew."* Gentle Lou is spacy and is very ticked off. He wants revenge. The robots won't tell him because while justice is supposedly being served Lou would find a way to extract his own. In going around public justice, he would be prosecuted. If Lou knew his toy isn't telling him he would wreck vengeance on the robot. He'd never let her off of the recharge stand. Bodily coordination and head trauma have defeated his goal to become a Marine. Roman fumes, *"Lou is screwed."*

Two other assassins also have unfunded contracts to hit Lorenzo and his friend. Both are still on their way. They still expect to get paid the balance due them from the scientists. Life would have been simpler for all involved if the clones they produced were able to handle this type of task. The people they replaced with a series of clones were knocked off by these very same assassins.

Sweet old Mom may be the epitome of goodness to Lorenzo and her children. No one would guess she also has a dark side. She's the widow of the famous, or infamous, sheriff of Buzzardville, depending on your ethics. Sis and Lou are his children with his sense of justice. With Lou still in recovery and Sis staying late at Lorenzo's after they visit Lou, Mom has taken to practicing her marksmanship at the tiny setup in the basement. They neighbors comment on hearing loud pops at night. When Mom is in the yard and they talk over the fence, this sweet gentle lady pretends she hasn't the slightest idea moaning. *"I wish they'd take all of their noise somewhere else!"* She really isn't fooling anyone. Old Buzzardvillains will say to one another in private, *"Everyone in this town knows everyone else's business." "Not forgiving or forgetting is in McPherson blood; you just wait."*

Her husband gave her the key to the locked cabinet in the cellar. She's careful to properly clean every weapon knowing, *"Clean gun; clean shot."* A fully automatic AR15 rests safely in her bed near where her husband slept so many years. It's clean as a whistle but Mom dares not use the automatic feature in the basement.

In her bathroom, just behind the toilet paper, a razor sharp knife is always ready. As a girl raised on farm just outside of town, she perfected her throw with this very blade. Her father always told his family, *"Might come in handy if any varmint comes at you."*

Sis and Lorenzo discover their intense attraction almost by accident. It happens without warning on their way back one night from visiting Lou. Their fingers touch and neither removes them. All of the kisses and hugs before were just play. A simple touch is for certain. Some may think an electric spark between lovers is just static electricity or even the ambient field around the world. Those who feel it know the truth. It's a light shining into their souls from heaven.

This realization is less complicated than the next step…talking about it. Neither can read the others' mind, So, the tone of their conversation now is softer and more serious. It will take something else to allow it to come into the daylight. But what!

Several days pass. When Lou focuses on their faces he become very calm and focused. He sees the way their faces have a brightness and a strange similarity of expression. For the first time since Lou was mugged and bagged he smiled. They look at his silly grin thinking, *"Poor Lou has gone completely over the edge."*. He blurts, *"When in the world did this happen?"* Both faces try to appear innocent. He laughs harder, *"You're both doing it again!"* Neither Sis nor Lorenzo understand because they can't see their own facial expressions. He tilts his mirror at them. *"Don't tell me you aren't in love"* *"It's on both of your faces like a big sign."* *"I approve!"* Lorenzo, finally laughs, *"That's good, I was afraid I'd have to kick your ass to get you to say that!"* Sis throws her arms around his neck saying, *"Renzo, I love you too!"* Lou hasn't lost his mind after all.

When Sis steps out to get something from down the hall, Lou asks, *"Renzo buddy, is this serious for you or just something else?"*

Lorenzo looks at him and admits he believes it's something meant to be. Lou, in total ignorance of his best friends wealth asks if Lorenzo shouldn't wait until he gets a real job after college to marry Sis. Lorenzo just nods and says, *"Lou, I'm not as poor as you might think." "My parents left me stocks." "Enough so if I never get a job, we'll be alright!"* Lou just shrugs in amazement. *"What did your mom and dad do?" "They made wise investments and they didn't spend a lot."* Lou knows Lorenzo well enough to know this is all he's going to say. Just then, Sis walks back in and they both go silent. *"What were you two talking about that's so sneaky that you clam up when I walk in?"* They both look away to avoid her gaze. Lou gratefully takes ta piece of candy from a bowl on the fireplace and rips off the wrapper. *"I plan to be out of therapy within a week!"* Just then a young woman about their age appears at the door. *"Therapy time."*

Sis texts her mother that she's Ok. But her mother is having problems of her own triggered by the attack on her son. Racoons have knocked over a flowerpot on the back porch and the noise makes

Mom think someone is trying to break in. She is sitting up in bed with her AR 15 and an ammo belt hung around her neck.

She whispers to the room, *"Bring it on!"* She drops off into such a deep sleep when Sis finally sneaks into the house just before dawn. She's so tired she doesn't wake up even when Mom removes her gun and ammo. Fortunately, it's Sunday and Sis doesn't have online courses. Mom awakens around noon to the scent of eggs and bacon coming from the kitchen. Sis yells, *"Come on down and eat with me!"* Mom realizes her face is dented from the imprint of the ammunition belt she slept on. She joins Sis and neither tells what they've been doing. Instead they talk about the Ravens football exhibition game coming up within the hour.

Lorenzo will join them just about game time. There is a knock at the front door. Sis says, *"It looks like Renzo's early!"*
She decides not to tell her mother for now of the change in their relationship. Terry moves quickly from her charging station in the same direction.

Angelbots

18

Justice

As Sis turns the lock the door is shoved open knocking her down her mother throws the butter knife she is holding at the intruders head as hard as she can. It would have bounced off harmlessly if Terry didn't calculate its' velocity and cut a tiny hole with her laser beam an inch in his frontal lobe. The thug doesn't speak or cry out. He leans over to help Sis up and hands her his gun.

He demands to know. *"Why am I here?"* Terry retreats back to her charging station unseen by Mom and Sis. Mom points to the snow on the sidewalk. *"You're here to shovel out sidewalk...with your shoes."*

As the assailant reaches the corner of the street, having completely cleaned the sidewalk up to the corner, his partner sees the blood running down his face and drags him and his shoes into the getaway car. *"What the hell happened?"* *"Why were you cleaning their damned sidewalk?"*

Holding his hand over the hole in his forehead, he pouts. *"You just said a bad word!" "That isn't nice!" "I'm going to tell1"* The driver grits his teeth and sputters, *"There's a band aid in my wallet; put it on your head; you're bleeding."* Here's my wallet." "Take it out of the middle part." Instead, the injured thug retrieves a condom and pushes it down over his head. The driver reaches for his wallet and realizes his partner has slumped down and his knees are touching the heater. The driver freezes in shock then runs through the red light.

The police stop him, Seeing the man in the passenger seat is dead having smothered, he tries to call in for an ambulance and a vehicle to transport the catatonic driver. He can't remember the appropriate police codes and just blurts into his microphone. *"Sheriff, I need somebody to call and pick up a dead dickhead and a blubbering zombie right now!"*

The coroner looks at the deceased and just shakes his head when asked whether it's a homicide. Dr. Kim refuses to speculate until the autopsy. One thing he knows, the gangrene in the victims feet hadn't had time and the butter knife wedged in his scull did not improve his health. *"A grown man commits suicide by placing a condom over his own head makes me think someone else held him down."* He suspects the subject suffocated. Even that is inconclusive. The police want to know if they should hold the driver. He nods affirmatively, *"Take him in for psychiatric evaluation and have the rental car returned because he's in no condition to drive and may not be for a while." "I suggest keeping in restraints."*

The Sheriff takes a statement from his cousin's mother. He places a screenshot in front of both, of each man. They immediately identify the one with Mom's butter knife. And have never seen the other one. After asking neighbors Lisa and Chris Flora. They both watched the deceased shoveling the sidewalk barefoot with his shoes. The sheriff finds one shoe. John and Eugenia Whitehurst who live just across from Mom, say they saw the man throw away his shoe and climb into the car. Mom wants her butter knife back, but Dr. Kim will not release it as it is now evidence. But no one dares accuse Mom, a native Buzzardvillain, of anything beyond losing her butter knife.

Terry, the robot, astonishes everyone by sending the police a video of the assault on Sis. Aside from Mom's unsolicited confession about throwing her blunt silverware at the deceased there is nothing on the video. Because a brilliant flash apparently from sunlight washed out the insertion of the object.

Poor Sis was still prone on the floor when the picture was taken. So she couldn't have reached the knife. Therefore she is ruled out. The sheriff and Dr. Kim cannot agree on how a blunt knife thrown from across the room could have so much force as to have pierced the skull. No charges are going to be made. Because there is no credible evidence a crime was committed.

When Lorenzo arrives at the house he finds Mom and Sis in tears and shaken. He recorded the Ravens game at his house and made Lou swear not to reveal the outcome until they can all watch it together. He calls on the old family home contractors from Catonsville to come and repair the damaged door. Both Sis and her mother will stay at his big almost empty home in Elkridge. At least until the they feel sure no one else is going to hurt them. Lou's almost recovered. He will remain at the big house with them. The engagement ring in his pocket is so large it's wearing a hole in his trousers. The two robots will stay behind to perform routine household chores. Both light up as soon as their human family goes out of the door. Neither tells the two young men who come to repair the door they are robots. Messing with the minds of humans is just too much fun.

Lorenzo wakes up with the realization today his friends are coming to stay. Mom and Sis have arranged enough of Lou's clothes and study materials in the room Lorenzo has set aside. Lou reenrolled in college.

He receives a call on his cellphone and sees it's Lou. *"Hi buddy, what time do you want me to come by rehab to pick you up?"* Lou sounds a bit puzzled, *"Someone I thought you sent already did."* *"I'm at the front door!"* Lorenzo opens the front door for Lou just in time to see a really big shiny black limo pull away. Lou says, *"The driver was a quiet uniformed chauffer, wearing a billed cap."* *"He showed up early saying he was sent by the foundation to bring me to your place."* Lou remembers his mother and father talking about similar things happening. But he doesn't remember much more than the word *"Zombie."* At this moment Lou's mom and sister bounce down the steps and embrace Lou with noisy enthusiasm. Both Dumas and Chippy sneak out back to escape the noise. The mysterious driver isn't spoken of again. For Sis and Lou, a zombie is just one more of Lorenzo's mysteries. Mom remembers a lot more especially the Wallow City caper, one that nearly ended her husband before his time.

Days pass, then weeks and the weather gets warmer. Lou's healing is almost complete. Chippy brought him up to date. His semester grades are equal to the others. Graduation is almost here, as are the nuptials for Sis and Lorenzo. When they left their house in Buzzardville in the hands of their robots, they left it for good. From time to time they stop by to check on everything but haven't the slightest inclination to return. No one discuses the odd situation they find themselves. Normal now is to leave two robots there. Because after practically begging for them, the twins lost interest. Only Chippy is a part of the family. She's even tolerated by Dumas.

The two robots live alone and no longer date the two young repairmen. The young men decided these girls were too platonic. And more into their work at some government agency to have romantic notions than them. No one in the neighborhood delves into their business because they weren't born and raised here.

After the two stop coming, it's politely assumed they are the type of women who would rather live without men in their lives. No talks about the affairs of others in this town. They leave each day for work in a government car and keep a normal workday routine. Back home around fiveish.

Their lack of garbage only seems strange to the sanitation workers who have never seen their trash cans. The opposite can be said for the recycle people. They produce only slightly less than the Whitehurst's and the Flora's combined. The poor soul who had the accident down the street in which his passenger died, came back once to sort out what happened to them. For no apparent reason, his accelerator jammed as he went past their house. He is permanently disabled and gets by on the little he receives from the church where he works as sexton. He walks with a great deal of difficulty.

On their wedding day they are somewhat surprised when the limo shows up at the door for Lorenzo and Sis is the same one that brought Lou home from the rehabilitation facility. Robert and the two estranged robots were invited and came to the wedding. They leave immediately afterwards; they were not invited to the reception.

Obviously, Lou was Lorenzo's best man. Mom lights both unity candles, one for her the other for Angela whose Lorenzo's parents are here in spirit only. The brides' side of the aisle is crammed with Sis's basketball teammates and competitors from several schools.

Father Kennedy doesn't ever remember seeing a taller more fit group of young women. As the they newlyweds proceed out of the church only Robert kisses the bride. But Lorenzo is kissed by every girl who attends the ceremony. Lou stands next to Lorenzo and kisses those girls as well. He get phone numbers from several. The reception is held at a very fine restaurant by the side of the river by the foot of venerable Buttermilk Hill. The ghosts of the Patapsco are also there. The spirits hang out with the ghosts and a good time is had by all. The sun is bright, and the flowers are a wonder to behold.

Back up at the house on the hill, Dumas and Hawk who obviously didn't attend the ceremony enjoy a piece of the wedding cake Hawk snatched and carried over the hill. Even a few crumbs fall and are gratefully scavenged by the omnipresent owl. Having been bested in every attempt to prey upon the raven who calls itself a hawk, the owl has become wise to the fact it never will win the battle.

There is a new lady of the manor. But for now the happy couple are off on honeymoon and won't be back soon. This leaves Mom to nurture her son. And no ghost nor demon dares come to call.

Angelbots

19

Terry

Robert worries his project is going to be discontinued unless something develops very soon. As the ambitious guy he is, he looks for ways his robotic assets can be more than fixtures. A friend discusses a problem he has justifying a clandestine operation involving a suspect. There isn't enough evidence for the utilization of a trained agent. So Robert digs into the massive surveillance library.

Based on satellite images, a house located just north of the Mason Dixon line next to the railroad repeatedly has people arriving and departing suspiciously at night. The frequency and method of their travel is alarming to both analysts.

The travelers wait for a CSX freight train to stop in front of the cottage. Then the suspect travelers climb on or off at will. It's completely normal for the train to stop whenever freight is shipped. A depot is just north of the site. The female robots are decked out in outdoor clothes and boots and sent to investigate the depot.

They carry very light backpacks with just enough contents to bear scrutiny if anyone detains them. Their only weapon is the laser wand. These wands don't need cartridges and are refueled by the same electronic field adapted to their own systems.

They have innocuous credit cards and fishing rods. If anyone asks, they will just tell them they like to fish. Obviously, they're twins. A nondescript vehicle transports them. All three have gotten drivers licenses. Their stated mission, as always, is to observe and report. Any sights and sounds near them can be amplified at the Agency.

A dark depressing place, the area is entirely industrial. Few might consider this no name part of nowhere to be a fishing destination. The dreary motel has a musty office and few decent customers. After checking into their room they immediately head for a spot in the river where no one would fish. It's just below the railroad bridge about a quarter of a mile from the house of interest. No one seems to be around at first. A miserable few find this to be an appropriate spot for nefarious transactions. Their activities aren't Agency business and definitely not a part of this assignment.

Back at the Agency, Robert views the lack of contact with pathos. Amtrak passenger trains pass frequently but still not a freight train. Robert realizes he has overlooked the CSX schedule. A quick check reveals none are due for several hours. He orders the *"girls"* as he calls them back to their rooms. They find their way back without incident and plug in. *"No sense in wasting a free charge whether or not you need one"*

A sleepy police car circles the parking lot. The officer takes note of the girls thinking they look a bit unusual for this area. But they aren't done anything wrong, so he rolls away. The police presence has deterred a hooded figure who trailed them from a distance in the darkness of the unlit night. This potential thug has no idea what danger he is in from them if he tries anything stupid.

Around three a.m. they are alerted a southbound CSX is due within the half hour. Both are charged up and head for the tracks at a pace a fast as an observer might expect of power walkers. Not too fast of slow. Reaching the bridge, they scale the side where its' supports touch the ground. Soon they find themselves next to a southbound CSX. One grinding gradually to a halt. They aren't seen by two individuals who jump off several cars ahead. Then run straight towards a shaded slowly blinking light in front of the house above the tracks. A high resolution clip is received and logged in at the Agency. As soon as the train begins slowly moving, two new figures run from the house and scramble onto the front end of a gondola. Robert instinctively orders his girls to climb onto the nearest gondola car and follow them south.

They do as told; In the morning, an agency employee will retrieve their car and fishing equipment. The room will be reserved for future use. The maid reports the absence of the evidence anyone used the room to management, including beds, soap, and toilets to management. The manager thought he had seen everything but happily announces, *"These young ladies are the best guests we've ever had."*

As those in the front gondola shiver in the predawn air, the girls make their way closer in an attempt to transmit their conversations. Reaching the top they are directly above looking down on two who shouldn't be there. Their language isn't one the girls have downloaded. This isn't a problem for Agency linguists. Sunrise finds the train halted for a crew change in a yard near Baltimore. The girls climb off of one side and are picked up by an Agency car. On the opposite side, two nearly frozen spies are hauled away in handcuffs. The Agency calls this synergism. Further down the line near Beltsville, another vehicle awaiting them will realize their loss and speed away in confusion.

Robert and his colleague will be allowed to continue surveillance. But will be criticized for failing to allow them to continue to their pickup site and on to others. The house by the railroad will continue to operate because it's too expensive for the parties who set it up to dismantle over just two operatives obviously caught by railroad police bumming rides. The area near the motel will be completely swept clear of night people by a branch of the State Police, responding on the basis of a report of criminal activities.

Only the local policeman puts the whole puzzle together. A sleepy one who noted to himself the girls on their fast walk were out of place and was suspicious. And he isn't telling anyone he observed suspicious activity and just ignored it. But the next time will be different. He realizes State caught the glory he should have nabbed.

The operators of the house by the railroad are in it only for the money. They aren't ideologically involved except for money. When freight trains are due to stop at the depot across the tracks, Homeland is notified from now on. The train stops just short of the area in a penned yard.

Any human cargo is unloaded before they reach the house. The same thing happens for those who get onto the freight cars as before. Soon the house is empty of transients and the owner closes shop and moves on or tries. The sleepy policeman has been watching the whole sting. When the owner starts to torch the building, this policeman camera records a very proper arrest for arson. *"I caught him in the very act of pouring the accelerant!"* He receives a promotion to sergeant. The officers under him hear his tale for years. Like all war stories, it gets better with repetition.

Robert and his Agency buddy try to get the Agency to buy more robots, rather than using those belonging to Lou and Sis. *"Plausible deniability,"* is the reason their idea is rejected. As long as robots can be *"borrowed,"* the Agency can deny any employee, or other assets are involved. The Director explains, *"We never know when someone here will become a turncoat, as has happened so often in the past." "We know these kids are loyal, but as our employees may seek employment elsewhere at will use what we teach them against us and the country."* So far a new permanent Director hasn't been designated, which is fine as far as the old/new temporary Director is concerned. *"It gets me out of the house."* Everyone laughs; few want to work midshaft.

Later in the evening, an Agency monitor picks up a cellphone conversation with encoded instructions to attack multiple Agency assets. A judge issues a release order for several of the freight passengers. As soon as they became free they blew the lid on the entire sting. They have banded with others terrorist groups to teach the Agency a lesson. However, their care in detention here is so much better than they had it at home, none want to be set free or returned to where they started their adventure.

As other groups join in there is no way to stop a sniper from killing a dozen employees entering the building in the morning. This threat simply wasn't relayed quickly enough to stop the carnage. A number of employees are killed including the two guards who witnessed Robert's dilemma. *"We win some and lose some,"* is all the Director can say when the casualties are counted at the post mortuum meeting.

The President issues a statement on all channels promising the American public, *"These cowards shall be tracked to the ends of the earth until they are found and punished." "No stone shall go unturned." "They will be caught and punished!"*

The federal judge who released the ones who disclosed the attack feels exonerated and justice was served. He followed the letter of the law and the rights of the accused were protected. *"No waterboarding on my watch." "The carrot prevails over the stick every time."* He will never acknowledge his judicial correctness was instrumental in the loss of irreplaceable patriots.

But, most importantly to him, his own name wasn't mentioned in the post mortuum hearing. . He tells his wife with a grin, *"I was just following orders!"* She listens without saying anything. Then goes to the bathroom and upchucks. Once alone he places both of his hands over his face and screams without making a sound.

It's impossible to pass the Agency without leaving a cam trail. The shooters are tracked to where they started. Electronic records tie then to an organization listed only as a hate group. Regardless of race, creed, or nationality this group hates all of humanity and wishes the land to return to its' natural state before the dawn of even early man.

They are all rounded up and released on bail. But they are intimidated to the point where most are neutralized. The frequency the robots left behind becomes eerily quiet. Then, one night it isn't, and Robert is asked to come into the Agency in the middle of the night. The system of codes used for the initial attack were broken belatedly.

This new threat targets an entirely different government facility, one located in the southwest. Robert can't reach Sis and Lorenzo for permission to use the girls. So he calls Lou for permission, Lou, readily gives his.

Just in case the action spills over onto her son, Mom has the girls load all of the arms and ammunition at her house into the car and brought to Lorenzo's where they now live. She calls her trusted neighbors, Lisa and Genie asking both families to keep an eye on her old home. And to call the police if they notice anyone suspicious nosing around. They focus their own security cameras on her house.

The girls pack no luggage. Everything they need is in the cargo hold of the new Agency 737Max. Stewards compliment them on their good taste in bullet resistant attire. The girls smile modestly and decline refreshments. They are fully charged and catalog everyone on the flight just in case the shooter or shooters are somehow traveling with them.

They are. Although they have no need to use the planes' restroom, both make several trips on the long flight. By the time, the plane lands two documented from earlier arrests are completely identified. Their hotel room is now bugged. There's only one problem: there are four hostiles reported within the warning. Two more are either on the plane or on their way to the same destination. And they are also females.

The girls have no idea the entire trip is a ruse designed strictly to capture them. Aware of the remaining unidentified adversaries, the twins try send information on every other passenger on the flight. Outside of the airport, with their luggage in tow they take an airport taxi to the same hotel as their two male targets. Two of the stewardesses bum a ride with them, as they also are staying at the Big Country Inn. The driver is pleased when the girls lift their own stashed luggage. Stewardesses have much less.

Every analyst back at the Agency Robert scans the two stewardesses just to be certain. Their identities are legitimate, except for one curious aspect…their eye scans do not match; it could be they have contact lenses. The girls are warned. Their conversation stops entirely…

The engine seems to be cutting out. The driver leans forward as though to be urging it on. Only Robert sees he is reaching for a revolver. Again, the girls are warned. As his hand holding the pistol come up and he points his weapon it becomes too hot to hold. And he drops it into one of the stewardesses laps. She screams. The car stops abruptly, and the driver jumps out. He's just local and didn't bargain for anything this weird.

But the car is his, in his confusion he tries to reopen the car door to get back in. It's jammed. He sits on the side of the road with his hands behind his head in resignation. The girls and the phony flight attendants sit waiting for something to happen.

It does. A helicopter appears to hover in front of the windshield. It's over without a shot having been fired. The driver will never hold much of anything in his burned hand. One phony stewardess will have the imprint of the revolver branded into her thighs for life. Still, they need the location of the upcoming attack. These two know the answer. The girls are determined to get it out of them. Robert turns off the feed to the Agency. They are on their own.

The girls appear to be nothing to worry about once the helicopter lifts off with the driver. This leaves the women to walk together up the hill to the hotel. They'll come back for the luggage.

To anyone watching the four might appear to just be four young women out for a stroll.

But their happy hike as they arrive at the place where a walking path down to the river crosses this road. All four solemnly turn down the path rather than towards the lodge. Both pairs exchange icy cold stares and step into the brush. All hell breaks loose. The assassins strike first by using their shoes as weapons across the girls' heads. The heels fly off into the air towards the river. The robots smile politely. Terry sternly warns, *"Young ladies, that will get you each a month in detention."* They are amazed by her nonchalant attitude. Two small revolvers come from hidden places. But the girls produce pointers that appear almost to be a joke.

As rapidly as triggers are pressed, pointers jam barrels. Terry points to the ground. *"Ladies, please be seated; we're going to chat."* And chat they do as they learn the attack is to occur at a supply facility not very far from where they are now.

Two women limp in front as they return to the car. One robot drives and the other keeps an eye on their two guests whose hair is woven to create one. They are conjoined at their heads and both have very sore feet from walking barefoot on sharp rocks.

Once Robert has them back in sight on his Agency monitor he records every part of their confession. Another chopper should arrive soon to carry them off to a place they won't consider a vacation destination. But that isn't what happens. Instead an official vehicle with three guards arrives not long before the chopper. With what appears to be an authorization to transport the prisoners. Tomorrow they will be found in the stream below with their heads still joined by their hair drowned.

Their spy masters were trying to stop them from disclosing the attack without knowing that cat is out of its' bag.

The helicopter that was to take them retrieves their corpses instead. It is evident to the Agency someone here is in cahoots with the organization that employed them. Internal Security is alerted.

Robert discusses the early detection of the girls with the Director. *"The stewardesses knew we were coming even before our girls did."* The Director tells Robert to discuss an idea he has with Lou and also with his sister and Lorenzo when they return from honeymooning. The robotic girls are in for an entirely new experience. Only if Lorenzo approves of an agreement with the Agency.

The following week finds Lorenzo and Sis back. Lorenzo receives a polite invitation from the Director for the newlyweds to stop across the road for tea. Sis quips, *"Tea can mean anything from we need help lifting something to let's go find more bad guys!"* Lou didn't mind being left out of the honeymoon trip because when the two lovers were away he followed the girls action. He's happy they're back though.

At ten minutes to four the following afternoon the couple ring the old directors' doorbell. They can hear the formal chimes and a shuffling sound from within. The door opens and they are ushered in and downstairs to the familiar quiet room. Robert and the current Agency Director are already seated at the table.

The Director presides over the meeting. *"We all have met previously, so I will get right to the reason we are here."* *"The Director and Robert have worked with two of your robots while you were away."* *"A penetration at the Agency creates the need for even more intense activity using these same mechanical wonders... but not right now."* Sis and Lorenzo sit stiffly in their folding chairs. *"Lorenzo, we want to employ you and Sis to serve as apparent inside employees of the Agency, but in reality as independent contractors."* Sensing a question, the Director goes on. *"Lou already has agreed to this idea pending your approval."* Lorenzo asks, *"What has this got to do with our girls?"* The Director nearly yells, *"We need to use them as bait!"*

This is the most sobering thought they've had since marrying. They look at one another. Sis nods. Lorenzo affirms. *"We're in agreement." "What do you want us to do?"*

Then a knock on the front door and another Agency employee enters the room. Robert opens the black briefcase at his feet and produces a contract. The Director goes on in one breath,. *"This contract binds you to provide janitorial service employees to the Agency as needed. We know you have a third robot...If my memory serves me, you call her Chippy." "In our present plan concept, Chippy will coordinate any data requirements with Robert on a daily basis from your home acting as intermediary because we can't have Robert seen talking constantly to Terry and Lucy." "We are pleased to offer each robot owner a sum as indicated."* Sis is highly impressed. Lorenzo sighs and nods his approval. Sis is glad her brother will have an independent income. Lorenzo still hasn't told his bride they are worth billions.

An Agency shuttle takes them to the building in the morning. They arrive at the same time as other applicants at a side building on the parking lot. They are tested and taken to lunch. Some applicants are sent back to waiting vehicles. Only the two girls are ushered into a room where their visitor badges change color.

Then they enter a classroom where an Agency instructor is waiting for them. They are sworn in as any humans would be. Instead of many months of training, the entire lesson plan is downloaded within one minute. The instructor certifies their learning. A new era of Agency employee begins. They are led to their new section to meet unsuspecting coworkers.

Their coworkers welcome them as they would human twins. To prevent confusion they are asked to dress a bit differently at work. *"No problem!"* They answer in unison.

At a required meeting in the morning, the Director puts it this way, *"In any organization so likely to be infiltrated by various enemies, there are people who are really the enemy." "Others are enemies of the enemy." Therefore we must have those* working for this organization who are spying on the spies." The Agency adds another layer of analysis to the registry of all three robots. Nothing in them still resembles the 9000 Series teaching aids from the factory.

The Director adds, *"Only Robert and I know the names of our internal security operatives." "They won't know you are robotic, or the fact you are not human." "To eliminate disclosure of who you really are, I have instructed our Security Section to simply report unusual activity where you are involved but not to physically intervene."*

It doesn't take long. By the end of the first week the Director is amused to receive a report about them from their immediate supervisor. *"Two new employees, who are twins, do not eat, drink or use the ladies room."* The Director receives permission from all of their owners to make slight modifications to the girls. Agency craftsmen aren't supposed to know how to modify robots, and a subsequent modification is made after the Director receives an update. *"The subjects now are eating and drinking in the ladies room." "One appears to have experienced a bladder problem in the cafeteria."* Their instructor is called back to teach them how to pee. Lucy keeps repeating at home, *"Nine thousands aren't supposed to pee!"*

Both are switched to another department with some modifications to their appearance. They no longer appear to be twins. In spite of disruptions, they each spot the internal security and report back to the Director. *"Subject individuals appear to be stalkers and possibly are dangerous."* The Director is beside himself and calls a clandestine meeting where he introduces the girls to his security team.

He states, *"We believe there are moles in this organization because these two young ladies were immediately spotted when I sent them on a mission to locate the headquarters of a group whose purpose is to provide support for our enemies." "They are apparently not affiliated with any single ideology." "The target group works for any and all who hire them from the dark web."*

Robert raises his hand thinking he's come up with the obvious solution. The Director waives him off, *"The obvious notion we should hire them is too simple."* *"We tried that; it won't work because whatever we pay them our enemies will top it on a contract by contract basis."* *"We have to identify them and take them out!"* *"It's just that simple."*

Robert is consumed with the idea someone or group within the Agency watches everything they do and selling it to the highest bidder. He calls his team together. *"We've had this problem before and beat it."* *"Look for those who seem to be looking at others who have no connection to their work and report back in one week."*

After a week, the girls have a long list…all involving people looking at the most attractive, including themselves in mirrors. He eliminates all of those and finds only several of interest. The Director moves positions around, supposedly to enhance evacuation, in case of a fire. The robotic ladies now find themselves supposedly working across from two suspects. Internal security people are in similar positions.

Both suspects are constantly talking to people outside of their own work group. The Director examines these and discovers that all but five are working on Agency sports. The five remaining have little or no reason to constantly interact. These suspects are followed, monitored, and have their work reviewed intensely. The Director is convinced he is on to something. A dummy bait leak is set up to test their loyalty. Four bite; one reports the vulnerability to his supervisor. One of the suspects the girls are watching is loyal. That leaves four.

Monitors are directed on these suspects. The robots follow them whenever possible. The four never meet with one another. Their comings and goings at home as well as their Wi-Fi at home is hacked. None are married or in serious relationships. It is though they live in a vacuum.

At last their communications network is discovered. It's timetable is when they're at work on a progressive schedule. Each day it advances by one hour and five minutes. All data is compressed and sent in an encrypted microburst the human ear would perceive as only noise. Each member of the cell has his encrypted code, one only their Control understands. Another protocol is used for rare times when Control determines it's necessary to simultaneously broadcast to everyone on the network. Those working on their Control transmit from an antenna disguised as a Purple Martin bird house. A high rise habitat for a mosquito lusting predator is a nearly perfect place to hide an antenna.

For a time this group makes no mistakes that might enable the Agency to learn where control is located. Triangulation of the broadcast signal leads nowhere. Out of frustration, the Director decides to prime the pump to create a reason for it to transmit. He creates a bogus project in which his Security people and one of the suspects are asked to monitor and report on robots. He informs the unknown robots are suspected of containing cloned organs. Both girls meet with them. The girls no longer resemble their twin or coworker personas thanks to Agency makeup artists. Lucy appears to be of Asian descent.

Although the adversary organization previously identified the girls as operatives, their appearances are altered beyond recognition. Even the shoe dents from the deceased flight attendants have been carefully removed. The Agency workshop used a small toilet plunger on each to suck the metal back into factory specs. Fortunately, their circuitry is undamaged. The Agency cosmetologist did wonders after their cranial dimensions were normalized. And more software was downloaded to improve vocal range.

When the girls were stationed near the subject she did some snooping. So, when one of the suspects left for lunch, Terry made it evident she was sneakily going over the details of his workstation. She keeps looking around to ensure no one could see her improvised stealth. This alarmed the suspect on the bogus team. As an honest Agency employee, he reported to the Director.

Another suspect did not because he might direct attention to his cohort. Instead he does what the Director anticipated; he reports to his subversive network. The Director has his network identity and confirmation of the cohorts' identity. This is a textbook tactic that was used to decrypt the Japanese codes preceding the World War II battle of Midway. Nothing is done; there's no value in tipping off the subversives with so little. The greater objective is to locate their tower and the who, what and where of the entire network.

While they don't presently know where to look for the remaining network, Agency data analyzers are churning the information gained into an improving profile. It is compared to all information in data storage from the earlier mission. Matched anomalies await more. The Security team sits poised like predators and wait. All are just breathing…very quietly, except the girls. Rather than stick out from the rest, both girls exit for the ladies room…because their new system requires they must go, or they will leak. And the truth is told they like to practice peeing.

At the big house on the hill where Dumas resides with Lou, Mom and the newlyweds things are quiet. The owl awaits patiently for Dumas to die so it can pluck out his eyes. Hawk comes and goes from the chimney top. And Dumas decides he and Hawk need to go hunt skunks. Owl understands and hopes Dumas gets sprayed by one of them stinking polecats. Then be made to lay outside in the rain. Hawk swoops down and plucks more wing feathers from one wing of the owl ensuring the fowl will become dizzy flying around in circles. A flock of vultures, thinking owl is one also, follow the owl around and around. Hawk tries to imitate Mr. Rogers by squawking, *"It's a weird day in the neighborhood."* Owl and buzzards just keep circling around and around...

Just inside of the walls, Sis, Lorenzo, Lou, and Mom celebrate Lou's birthday. Today they are oblivious to everything beyond the happy walls of a really big old house. Even the ghosts in the cellar and attic sing along with their own memories of candles and cake. Somewhere far above the souls of Lorenzo's departed parents sing for Lou too.

Angelbots

20

Ghosts

"If tell children your ghosts aren't real it becomes a big problem when you later try to explain the Holy Spirit." Sister Carol is counseling a group of new teachers at the convent school. A class that includes Courtney, Bianca, Morgan and Drea. Sister Albina observes and bemoans there's not a single *Mary* among this motley crew. Then Mr. Connor, the school's religion teacher, pokes his head into the classroom. *"It's all a matter of faith he announces with his voluminous voice." "Faith is the umbrella of the soul."* Just as swiftly, his figure dodges out of sight.

Mr. Connor and Sister Carol were great friends in school because they shared a love of the Lord but wanted a vocation devoid of having their own children. Like so many others, they wanted to focus on God and his church. Little do they realize they are about to experience the wrath of demonic forces of hell within walking distance of where they serve.

Newlyweds, Lorenzo, and Sis were married in this church just a month ago. The parish overlooks a river where there is a temporarily sealed passage to hell. It has been used in the past by immortals, including the Grim Reaper, to force down those whose evil couldn't otherwise be contained. His mother once narrowly missed being killed by one of those demons at this very spot and was saved by the Grim Reaper.

When he walked the earth the demon was the murderer known just as Strangler. He was a force so evil it took Gee, as the Grim Reaper likes to be called, everything in his power to subside and send down his soul. It has been in hell for two decades yet relentlessly attempts to return and destroy.

He cannot except through earthly minions. He presses upward craving the blood of Lorenzo. He is the son of the one who was able to recover her body and soul from his grasp. Hawk senses his evil is brewing again and warns Dumas to be vigilant and watch over Lorenzo. And his friends Lou and Sis with every bit of strength his poor old doghide can muster. Hawk heads off to report to the angels.

They react to any threat involving demons instantly. They will implore an army of angels for a good life for the newlyweds without the presence of demons. An underworked guardian angel assigned the good priest on the hill is also petitioned. And she responds that the good minister has a full schedule at the moment.

Today Mr. Connor is more interested in praying for the souls of the departed today. Sadly, the moment has passed. Early the following day the priest gets underway. His Jeep chugs up the hill to perform the blessing. The evil demon is already at the doorstep. But the demon remembers he's been to this place and the outcome was disastrous.

"What happened?" the demon tries to remember but he's been in hell so long his mind is fried. Mr. Connor beats him to the

punch. *"In the name of God, be gone from here and all who dwell withing!"* The demon loses his advantage trying to remember. Hawk jokes. *"Close caw."*

There is no program in the robots to keep it from being possessed by a demon. And so losing the humans within it slides into Chippy. She's in danger of being possessed. But still the demon can't cross the blessed thresholds of the house due to the blessing. Although Strangler remains in hell a virus of his mind is controlling the demon who is now Chippy. Maybe this demon was a good choice in the sick mind of Strangler's soul. The human it came from was destroyed while trying to break into this very door. For a moment, the demon sees himself just inside laying dead. A fierce animal tearing him apart while Lorenzo's late mother pulled the trigger of a gun she just fired. His recollection of the pain is unbearable.

In total panic the demon escapes from Chippy in terror. He sees the same dog coming after him. Dumas snarls at the evil creature. The demon says to no one, *"This isn't supposed to happen; how is it any living creature can see me?"* The dog presses forward and the demon runs as fast as can for the relative safety of hell. Then, as the animal charges the demon retreats to the pathway in the river and seals it behind him. The ghost of old Will Gold seals it from the upper world side. This is what he's been waiting for. Then he's gone. Dumas is happy! The angels sigh in relief. Chippy receives an antidemonic inoculation. Chippy's become the first demon proof robot in eternal history.

The angels return to their regular assignments. Dumas and Hawk trot and ride along the beautiful river. Lorenzo, Sis, Mom and Lou play monopoly again. And Lorenzo gets around to asking Mom whatever made her name his wife who everyone calls Sis, Martha? Mom ignores his question says, *"Not so much talk; Just roll the dice!"*

As Robert watches the events of the evening from his station at the Agency in the morning he will only see what a living being should know about spirits and demons, for no living person can know what only the immortals know. He saw nothing unusual. Neither did Mr. Connor. For some reason he can't explain, from now on he will pray for the souls of the living before the faithfully departed.

Just as easily as Sis and Lorenzo fell in love and married the girls, although robots, have blended into their roles as Agency employees. The neighbors see them come and go so routinely; they have all but forgotten the drama of the contractors. Even that poor soul who shoveled the sidewalk with his shoe. And when they analyze happenings at the Agency they must adjust to the time variance between the actual events they shared in communication with Chippy's demonic threat and that recorded. People find it much easier to be deceitful than machines. So, the angels rewrite their data for them. As Ralph explains, *"Time differs from earth to angels."*

The remaining suspects now need to be verified. The girls are conveniently reassigned when the suspects are quietly detained. Oddly, they don't demand legal representation. They simply swallow pills they were provided for such an occasion. They didn't work for a foreign power who might swap spies for them. For they, like their organization, are just in it for the money. Their disappearance from the Agency puts the rest in a state of panic. They manage to pull the big plug. All systems go dark. But the girls don't mind.

They never get tired or bored. They cling so closely to their targets, that the targets start depending on the girls and start dating. The dates aren't much though because everyone has a big secret.,, who they really are. Bowling is a big date. The two couples are at the same place and time so often, they seem to strike up a friendship. It's ironic because both couples know one another way too well. And bowling is something to do until things work themselves out. Clandestine spying is sometimes compared to watching grass grow.

More and more the girls listen and bring out the details of their partners hidden meanings behind sly remarks. Bored Robert has to listen to what he considers drivel each morning.

This conservative analyst decides to exhibit his impatience to the Director. By growing a beard and refusing to have his hair cut until the suspects resume their nefarious deeds. The Director doesn't bother to ask for updates and Robert's hair gets longer and longer. At last one day the Director realizes Robert has a buzz cut and is clean shaven. The game is back on!

The downbeat of a perfect strike is music to the ears of any bowler. The girls were cautioned not to attract attention by ever rolling perfect games. For the sake of their mission they allow their partners to win most. A precision machine has a bias to bowl strikes while their human counterparts seem to have the opposite. The subjects have become increasingly careless in their comments about those other activities.

One great night they all happen to bump into some of the others in their wicked enterprise. The others mistakenly think the girls are OK to openly discuss things. Several places are mentioned before the subjects can shut them up. A deafening silence follows. *"We can't take chances they are going to tell someone."* It's agreed to bump off both on the way to taking them home. Because they came in separate cars, each man will murder his own girlfriend. As one puts it, *"All neat and tidy!"*

Robert is nearly asleep when his phone alerts him. He calls an emergency number. Agency security has wheels rolling by the next frame. Although the suspects know the girls live together, one makes an excuse to stop by an ATM to get some cash. *"This will only take a minute."* He pull under the bank canopy, stopping just before the machine. Grabbing a revolver as he steps out, he aims, presses the trigger but nothing happens.

Holding his bullets in one hand that she holds out. She asks innocently, *"You need these, don't you?"* Grabbing at them he gets a fistful of empty shells. Very quickly she emptied each one. *"Little boys shouldn't play with such dangerous toys!"*

He tries to drag her out of the car. She cooperates. Squeezing her pretty neck with all of his strength, he fractures four fingers. Just then, a black car pulls up behind them. The driver flashes his badge. *"What seems to be the problem?"* Suspect one stutters, *"Nothing officer, just a lovers quarrel."* The Agency officer still pretends to be a County police officer, *"I'm sorry sir, but your date seems to have passed out!"* The robot is laying on the ground pretending to be dead.

Seeing no way out, the suspect pulls a knife and starts to slash the officer when an innocent looking wand points at the weapon. The knife melts into the screaming suspects burning hand. He's easily subdued, and the bleeding stops as the wound is cauterized. Shock sets in as they shove him in the back of the trunk. All he can think to say, *"Tell them at work I'm taking a week off because I am taking sick leave!"* He won't be losing sick leave because he will find himself at work in morning. Under heavy medication he explains the entire mercenary network where it is and who's involved. After this confession he will reside in an even more secure place far away. Next, for suspect two...

The prospective killer and victim each watch as the other car peels off for the ATM. Neither comment on the departure. He places his hand on her leg and is surprised at its' firmness. *'You seem cold."* She's programed to suitably respond and does, *"Cold hands, warm heart."* Although it wasn't her hand he touched, he takes it as a sign she's submissive. That plays right into his plan to get rid of her. She knows she said something misleading and can't think of a way to set it straight without losing control. Her internal logic is warning her she is in danger.

He heads toward a popular spot overlooking a historic railroad station. She's completely quiet, unwilling provide another miscue. The car stops on an abandoned parking lot just out of public view. His door opens; he sits on a rock wall. Then he motions to her to come look down over the valley below. The fate of her partner comes in.

Still she comes close to him and as she arrives at his side he scoops her up and pushes her over the wall. Hooking his arm, together they glide out over the treetops. *"Why did I allow him to do that to me?" "It isn't logical."*

Two spies locked in a death grip sail downward. She points her laser straight down to hopefully cushion the impact. Instead it only prolongs the inevitable by pushing them along the surface of the river until eventually they hit a wire and sink to the bottom of old Will Gold's lake..

Angelbots

21

Reality

Images and recordings received by Robert from the bowling alley are enough to trace the other mercenaries back to their lairs. Coupled with the burnt blabbermouth in Agency custody, any who may have gotten away are finished. Without the eyes and ears of the suspects, including one who drowned, there is no longer an organization. The Director, quotes his favorite old TV show, *"It's over Robert, book 'em!"*

The Director points out to Robert, *"We owe Lorenzo's foundation, or someone, a whole lot of money for the modified 9000 robot."* Thinking better of it, he tells Robert to bring them all in here for the memorial service. *"We can't give up the fact this whole thing was a sting operation and that girl who everyone here thinks was a person, isn't really human."*

The three robot owners, the Old Director and even Mom assemble once again in the meeting room just off of the Directors' office, along with the robots Terry and Chippy.

No tears are shed for the robot. And no one knows exactly where in the water the missing person and Lucy have disappeared.

And no one will. Because, neither the robot nor the drowned suspect will surface for a while. An Agency medical examiner speculates he will eventually come up, but she won't. *"Metal doesn't float unless it's a part of a boat."*

The Agency will go on; the code breakers will decipher. For now Mom and Terry will live at Mom's old home. Not a soul in their neighborhood will notice that Mom has replaced the robot as they each leave for work each morning. Their minds fill in the blanks. It's all life as usual. But Mom still sleeps with her guns. And her sharp blade sits next to her in the bathroom. No more dull butter knives for protection.

Lou comes into a windfall. Agency accountants adjust his robots' present value, including all the improvements, subtract the Agency software and upgrades. Add back in the accumulated rental, plus salary. Then there is the group life insurance. The policy doesn't exclude robots. Even without it, Lou will still have enough to pay off his college loan and start a business of his own.

The day of the memorial arrives. Obviously, the dead suspects' family arrives at a local chapel. No bodies were retrieved, so no need to explain why one might be rusty. Mal Fidler limps in and has tears in his eyes explaining how sad he is that his son Gary never had a family. Elderly Grace, his grandma, is wheeled in and is even more distraught. She grips Mom's hand and comforts her with the knowledge she is sure her *"daughter"* is with the Lord. Mom just bows her head with shame at her deception.

The Director is equally devious as he eulogizes the virtue and hard work of each of these young Agency employees. Several others also arrive and are promptly cataloged by Terry. She doesn't shed a single tear...because she doesn't know how; it isn't programmed within her.

Everyone is invited back to the Agency cafeteria for lunch including the newly cataloged mourners. While their eyeball scans are discretely collated. No one directly corresponds to anyone, but on further analysis they are with another investigative agency. Robert knows more about the deceased by the time lunch is over than anyone has learned to date.

As everyone leaves, he and the Director head back to their offices with new input. Mom and Terry ride home. And Grace and

Mal head on back up to their home in the mountains. When Lou, Lorenzo, Sis and Chippy arrive back at the big house they are greeted by Dumas.

The old dog sniffs and the hair on his neck rises. A very old scent of hated Mal comes with them. He once saved Lorenzo's dad from a savage beating by Mal and his departed friends. Hawk looks down from the chimney whispering, *"Forget it Dumas: it's all just water over the dam now."*

Dumas doesn't understand gallows humor but instantly forgets his anger looking up a tree, *"I wonder if Owl tastes good?"* Hawk laughs. Owl takes off in circles again. No one chases the owl. Even the buzzards have left the big house on the hill.

And within the big happy home Lou, Sis and Lorenzo play Monopoly. No angels allowed. The game is the only thing the real people can do as well as their robots. Chippy and Terry only for a microsecond start to feel the loss of their rusty friend. But then robots are merely mechanical creatures… aren't they?

The Agency roundup of those who planned the ambush of Agency employees on a dark day continues. The information vendors are gone but those who paid them are still out there. The President and those loyal to traditional ideals will continue the search if it takes forever. The President states once again, *"This is not a country where violence against the institutions of the people is forgotten or forgiven." "We will follow treachery to the end of the earth."*

Wherever one goes, the electronic surveillance increases without an end in sight. Gradually the puzzles are merging into a vast mosaic involving many groups. Some of which despise one another. Some are domestic home grown. Others are from foreign interests. Both government and mercenary organizations are of interest to the Agency. In a free society, the new recruits come to work here with their own slant on right and wrong. The problem is- how to prevent the next sneak attack. Governments must resort to ways of learning threats with methods that just sound wrong. Especially to those who arrive without an understanding of history. Preservation of any society is a rocky road when there is division, according to the Director.

Traditional adversaries of the Agency have taken the internal ruminations of the country as opportunities for mischief. There is no more destructive traitor than one with a sterling past. Barry Parker is a perfect example.

Barry had a great Navy career and even managed to get hit by a fragment during a mistaken attack involving friendly fire. In the course of midlife he has become vulnerable to younger women. This wouldn't matter much if Barry didn't have so sensitive a job in the Agency as the Clearance Officer. Barry knows the good, bad, and ugly about everyone who works here. The position allows him to choose whether to pull an offenders clearance. Or like a father confessor, forgive and judge transgressions as minor. He was promoted to this position after his success with Robert in taking down the clone factory. Until a suitable replacement for his old job is trained he is holding down two Agency positions. When he's off somewhere, Robert answers his phone.

Recently Barry has taken to lying to his wife about his whereabouts after work. It started as a beer or two at the Agency waterhole. The Half Mast is about a mile from the front gate and has the murky atmosphere of similar water holes throughout the world.

Barry's favorite spot. A back corner where he can see the door and everyone who walks in. Tonight there are two young women seated quite close. He carefully slides into his corner. His favorite whiskey, *Old Forester*, instantly appears before him. The bartender gives him a knowing look and half smile and walks back to the front.

The two women appear unaware of him until he takes out his wallet and lays down a twenty. His Agency badge has slipped out of his shirt where it usually stays tucked on the way home. One woman bids goodbye to the other and leaves.

For about ten minutes both pretend to watch a Capitols recap on the wall, then she looks at him saying *"Go Caps!"* He realizes she has no idea what she is saying because the clip was of the Penguins scoring. He looks her over and realizes she's flirting. In his deepest voice he tells the bartender, *"Give the lady whatever she's drinking."*

As the evening passes, she moves closer leaning in towards him and touches his hand from time to time. Her perfume is pleasant yet not overwhelming. His drinks keep coming but she hardly touches hers. He never makes it home.

Waiting at home, his wife is frantic. She has suspected him of cheating for some time. Her life is in shambles and she has sought help, but it isn't. She calls his old duty phone. It rings and rings until finally Robert happens to pick it up. She asks to speak to Barry. Robert innocently explains, *"Barry left hours ago with the day shift just as I was coming in," "I haven't seen him since then,"* It never occurs to him straight and somber Barry would be out screwing around. She sighs dejectedly saying, *"I thought as much." "Tell him I called and that I have always loved him."* Dense Robert simply jots her message on a pad for Barry to find whenever he gets back. The thought this lady is about to commit suicide never crosses his mind.

As Robert's shift is ending in late morning two Agency security officers arrive and unfold a black cover over Barry's station. Robert asks, *"What's going on?"* One is looking at the message.

"She took her life last night." "He was located this morning with a foreign spy." Robert feels the blood drain from his head and flops in complete shock. His coffee mug crashes to the floor in pieces. Like the mug he will never recover. Reality is a bitch.

Robert will remain with the Agency for many years and then retire. However, his self confidence will never be complete. He should have foreseen a call from a wife at that late hour required more than a simple answer. Anything he said would have been better than telling her the truth. With some modification, no matter how slight, at least she might be alive.

Back at the big house on the hill, life proceeds more casually. Lou is asleep on the couch. The newlyweds are snug in their bed. Old grey Dumas snores in the corner with his legs running as fast as his dreams. While up on the chimney Hawk watches and observes the poor owl circle and catch a very slow mouse. As he watches, the tattered owl is approached by a demon with who offers owl possession for power.

The owl screeches *"GET OUT!"* and the demon is gone. Hawk is impressed as the owl, who is worse for wear, had an opportunity to become whole and even more. So, Hawk will ask the angels for a proper reward for this inelegant fowl. No virtuous act should be unrewarded.

When the old dog is out on the lawn again Hawk explains all he saw. So they awaken the owl and tell him he is their pal. From now until his feathers grow out they will share their visceral harvest. To help him fly straight once more Hawk gives him several of his own feathers. Owl is astonished.

Mom and Terry the robot settle down in the home where Sis and Lou grew up. Mom is determined to help Terry develop a human personality although they haven't much in common. Terry doesn't help the matter by telling Mom her soap opera is inaccurate and unrealistic.

Mom tries to counter by throwing the circuit breaker on the wall plug where Terry supposedly recharges. It simply doesn't work. No one taught Mom about Tesla's ambient energy field. She calls Lou in panic; he soothes her fears. Just the same, poor Mom starts locking her bedroom door and wears her bullets to bed.

Dumas learns of Mom's concern and he tells Hawk. And of course Hawk tells the angels. They in turn worry some of their mind transfer to the robots has caused a problem. A scan of the Terry and Chippy confirms their suspicions. Robert still monitors them as well.

He notices unusual activity but hasn't the slightest idea what. He's no longer on good terms with the Director and doesn't want to start something that might get him terminated. He just watches and waits for anything new.

Angel Ralph is chosen by his wife Lucien, also his boss, to temporarily repossess Terry. If Mom knew her robot was possessed she would panic so around the house it's business as usual. That means Angel Ralph, as Terry, carries out the trash.

This continues for over a week without his wife's quelling force on Ralph's adventurous nature. Ralph decides to wander around the neighborhood after Mom is asleep. He will ensure no riffraff bothers the good people. Ralph doesn't realize why he has this urge. But his amused wife understands only too well for she recalls her Ralph once was none other than Vigilante Spirit, a seeker of justice.

As Ralph wonders the backstreets in the robotic body of a lovely young lady he's aware he is a perfect one angelbot sting operation for meandering night stalkers. He wonders far from Moms' and into unsavory places. He reaches the habitat of the unholy. Like a fisherman he reels them screaming. He doesn't take human lives for that is against all that is holy. But some will wish they were dead when his laser surgery heals. There is no recidivism among those who can't keep lust to themselves.

He follows a group onto a bus whose banner states it is going to Wallow City. Because he hasn't money to pay the fare, he must slip past the conductor by temporarily freezing his mind. Then quickly to a seat behind a gaunt woman with two young children. While the girl stares at nothing through a window her younger brother is constantly in motion. The tiny child keeps insisting, *"Me hongy!"*

A nondescript man sits across the isle from them. It's obvious his eyes are on the mothers' big open bag. The angelbot is ready to paralyze the hand as soon as it reaches to steal anything. Instead, the man reaches into his own wallet. He takes out all that he has, a twenty dollar bill. Then, deftly slips the bill into the womans' bag. The woman seems not to notice. The single tear running down her cheek gives her away. The angelbot is in awe. This homeless individual just gave away all of the money he has in the world.

From a distance, the angelbot follows him to an alley that was reclaimed several years ago as a part of the Wallow City revitalization project. It was called Lizard Alley back then. The man finds a niche at the edge of a building and uncovers his few personal belongings. Fortunately, he has a bottle of water to sip away his pangs of hunger.

As a building tenant moves past him, averting his eyes and holding his nose, a light appears in his mind. This normally discrete individual opens his wallet and presses three twenties into the mans shirt. The recipient is overjoyed and says, *"God bless you sir!"*

The man turns back to the homeless one offering, *"Could you use a bath and some clean clothes?"* The angelbot smiles for the first time ever but her paint doesn't crack. Ralph realizes, *"Lizard Alley, you've come a long way since I was last here!"*

The man phones his wife as they enter the building. Although she sounds calm over the phone she cringes at the idea of bringing the stench of an unwashed body into their home. By the time she greets them at the door, she has stopped shrieking and is polite.

A line of towels on the floor leads to the bathroom and the shower is running. A good set of her husbands' underwear, socks, clothing, and shoes awaits this man once showered. Dinner will follow.

The homeless one showers. The warm water and fragrance of the soap bring back memories of a kinder time in his life. Unlike many of his fellow knights of the alley he didn't lose his fortune to drugs and alcohol or even unkind mental issues. His downfall is his complete generosity leaving no means of his own.

As the angelbot waits in the alley, the angel observes all from within the room as the three diners enjoy their meal. The wife is shocked to see how refined her guests manners are. As he toasts her elegant fare with his water glass she decides, *"This is a prince in disguise!"*

The possessed robot leaves for home on a return trip of the same bus. This time the driver is more alert. He realizes the lady getting on is moving every time his eyes blinks shut because a lady in the front laughs hysterically. By the time he can say anything though his mirror is fogged. Ralph leaves a suggestion in Lorenzo's mind. *"Send a nice donation to the bus line to cover those who cannot pay."*

A cold wet puppy shivers just behind a policeman at the next stop. Neither the officer nor the driver notice the puppy just behind the officers' heels. As the driver and the officer exchange good words, the laughing lady who saw the robot pass roars with joy. As the puppy passes her on it's way down the isle it does what dogs do to dry off as if to yell, *"Snitch!"* The laughing lady says something back that sounds the same but isn't.

Pooch and robot meet for the first time. Ralph says, *"I can see you were dumped."* Pooch admits, *"Yeah, I got tossed because the cat framed me!"* *"How'd that happen?"* Ralph asks.
"Cat was jealous and wanted me gone." *"Whenever I'd take a nap that cat would spread litter box stuff all over me!"* *"Really?"* The angel asks. *"Did you ever dig in the cats' litter box yourself and throw stuff all around?"* Dog mumbles, *"Maybe."* Then the puppy starts snoring pretending to be sound asleep. Ralph laughs.

Stopping predators brought it to this point. Feeding the homeless, sending home lost souls and even lost animals is a is ideal. When it isn't practical to return to a place without kindness it leads them to a place of respite. Ralph just wants to do the work of the

Lord. Ralph realizes he better get the robot home or Mom will blow her top.

Mom is awakened by scratching at the door. A very dirty little puppy looks up at her and it's love at first sight for both. While she feeds it her leftover stew Ralph slips Terry back onto her charging station and relinquishes control. Once more, the robots realize everything. Only Robert, who wouldn't be able handle what Ralph and Terry have done together as an angelbot, isn't aware. He and Chippy are aware that Mom has a new puppy.

Ralph has an idea. Because so many commercial buildings are becoming vacant, the result of virtualization, why can't they become places for people like the man in Wallow to sleep. Why must some people have no where to shelter except out in the element in niches and hollows? He has just to the person to inspire.

Lorenzo wakes up just before dawn. He gets out of bed quietly so as not to disturb Sis. Who doesn't awaken him anymore. He's just had the weirdest dream. In it his foundation, which he barely notices, buys suitable empty commercial buildings. Then converts them to become habitats for the homeless. He doesn't have any idea who the homeless really are. So, over breakfast, he and Sis discuss the idea. She is all for it; again she has no idea who they are either. *"Why don't we ask our friend Mr. Connor?"* They make an appointment through Mary the rectory housekeeper.

The Paster, Mr. Connor and the couple are of one mind. They sit down over tea at the rectory and brainstorm. *"How do we keep it from being a place for those who are evil at heart?"* Sis asks. The priest nods wisely, *"There's a thin line between a noble effort and a good idea subverted."* Lorenzo chips in, *"Selectivity is the answer."* The priest suggests, *"We could pole the charities of all faiths to learn who are the innocently afflicted."* They agree.

Sis has the most interest in organizing. And she sees a good chance to finally put their robot to good use. *"It has been doing practically nothing except for a few Agency tasks."* *"Why don't we bring her and Mom back here?"* Lorenzo misses Mom's cooking. Her daughter has a long way to go to catch up. But he never says as much to Sis. She calls Mom. Her mother is enthusiastic. *"I will only stay with you if I can bring my puppy!"* Sis doesn't ask Lorenzo, she just says, *"Yes."*

Dumas has heard and is screaming *"No puppy!" "No, no, no!"* To everyone in earshot if sounds like *"Go, go, go!"* He runs outside and yells it to Hawk and even to owl. They both fall off their perches laughing. *"Dumas is getting a partner!"*

Mom and her puppy arrive with Terry carrying the luggage. *"Puppy"* the only name Mom wants to call it, sniffs out Dumas…tries to hide behind the shoes in an upstairs closet.
But his tail banging on the wall gives him away. Although Puppy isn't grown, he has huge paws. Dumas shivers in trepidation as the big footed monster comes nearer and nearer to his closet.

Mom decides that her old house can serve a good purpose as a part of Lorenzo's idea. It will be a place for the people who are managing the first facility. They need a place to get away from the place they work. It doesn't take long for the priest to provide a list of candidates for Lorenzo's foundation. Now for the location and staff.

Lorenzo calls on a real estate firm specializing in large commercial structures. He informs the Secretary of his foundation of his plans and asks how much he can afford to spend. He doubles up in shock to learn there are billions available. He tells the realtor to start big. Within hours nearly abandoned shopping malls all over the country become possibilities.

Lorenzo assembles his committee at an old meeting hall in Elkridge. The commercial realtor is first speaker. He shows slides of the shopping malls most suitable. They each have beautiful tile floors and are highly secure with internal monitoring systems. Each is available for pennies on the dollar compared to the cost of rebuilding the same structure. But they have outlived their purpose as retail structures because the internet has brought about newer means of distribution. So called brick and mortar stores are diminished as places people wish to buy things on the internet.

To kick off the project, Lorenzo buys a beautiful but obsolete mall in nearby Buzzardville to use as a model. Old store fronts give way to a hotel like interior. Residence fronts are massed produced and shipped to the sites where they are carpentered to fit. Interiors still have the same expensive tile as before. Empty malls become a first class apartments. Plumbers and electricians from all over the country come to work and marvel at the improvements.

Back in Wallow, the homeless man is reluctantly persuaded to attend church with the man and woman who took him in from the alley. The homeless one's benefactors support him as he unsteadily climbs the church steps.

They walk into the church; the homeless one tries to shield his face. *"Mr. Man welcome!"* The pastor greets them with a warm welcome. *"Brothers and sisters, I want you to welcome the brother whose generosity enabled this church to be built in the first place!"* At first everyone stares at the embarrassed man and woman sponsoring the homeless one. The pastor makes certain everyone realizes it is the man in a secondhand suit and the hang down expression. He gave everything he had to the church. everything he owned.

When he listened to the homeless one's story, the minister submitted the form he had just received from Lorenzo's foundation. The homeless man is the first tenant of the newly formed home in the mall. When Lorenzo hears his story, the man is the one who cuts the ribbon. He's no longer homeless.

Angelbots

22

Lost

Robert at the Agency thinks he knows where he can find his missing robotic asset and the suspect, Malcolm, Jr. Since they suddenly disappeared from view several months ago he has been searching with every tool they have. Air and ground turned up nothing.

Coming up with just zero, Robert's tenuous relationship with the Director has gone from bad to worse. Finally, he has a hunch that requires the Directors' approval. When he hears Robert wants a meeting, he thinks optimistically, *"Hurrah, maybe he's turning in his resignation."* But, when Robert is seated before him with a chart, he dejectedly realizes he's wrong. Robert clears his throat nervously.

"Sir, I need your approval to contact the local police dive team." The Director rolls his eyes wondering why. Robert doesn't wait for an answer. *"We have been looking too far upriver."* *"They must be here."* He points to a dam not far from the home of Lorenzo and his family. *"Isn't that on the property of the people from whom we leased the robots?"* Robert nods pointing to the exact spot where the dam is on the chart. *"Exactly!"* The Director rubs his chin. *"Go ahead."* *"But do not tell them anything about a robot."* *"Just say we are interested in knowing what the contour of the bottom looks like."*

Robert agrees and starts by letting Lorenzo know they are conducting a search of his lake. And not to be alarmed by the presence of police vehicles. Lorenzo is agreeable but decides to look in on the project when the time comes. So does Dumas as well as Hawk.

The dive team arrives in two vehicles. One has an air generator and scuba equipment. The other has the personnel.
It takes about a half hour for the team to hack their way through several decades of overgrowth to a small platform. The pier is remarkably intact although it has been unused for so long. Two divers

go in and acclimate to the cold. Two more sit on the pier ready to assist.

Suddenly those in the water break the surface tugging the arm of Malcolm, Jr. Although they have him by the arm, something seems to be holding him down. A line is used to hold his body until they can get a better grip. A call is made to headquarters for the coroner and a tow truck. The divers stop and wait. Dumas just sits in wonder. Hawk chases an annoying crow from the area then returns to wait with Dumas.

Then the silence is broken by a distant siren that grows increasing louder and then stops. Doors slam, footsteps draw near. Lorenzo watches from atop a hill. No one says a word. People are moving toward the pier with a sense of foreboding. The tow truck chains rattle over the ground and a sling is attached to the end.

The second group of divers enter the water. The sling passes down to the one holding the limp dead arm. The arm falls back as the sling supports his body. Oh so slowly the chain is retrieved by the truck link by link as the body slides towards the pier. Still something heavy still drags the body down. They do not dare to pull harder. And then a metal fist appears. It remains clenched around the leg of the corpse. It can't be budged.

The first chain is removed. The sling is secured, and the chain is attached to a second sling. The leading diver moves deeper into the water and attaches this sling to the really hard body of a young woman gripping the leg. Her face is animate, her skin and her eyes seem alive. Her skin is as firm as the body of the man she grips is not. The diver shivers in fear as he looks into her eyes.

The line is attached, and he comes up and swims to the pier with his buddy close behind. Those on the pier help both divers out and they are guided to a warm vehicle as more vehicles arrive.

Robert watches from one of the newly arriving vehicles. *"The Director isn't going to like this one damned bit!"* The police agree to limit access to the area. Lorenzo taps on the window. Robert opens the door to let him in. Lorenzo smiles, *"I see you've located our missing girl."* Robert just winces. *"We have an Agency ambulance on the way to carry her back."* *"Hopefully, a recording will show what happened."*

Hawk doesn't need a recording to know a robot influenced by angels has killed a human being. It's something that's never supposed to happen. His observation falls flat first in a ruling from Heaven and a month later in a similar finding from the Agency. Heaven sees the fatal grasp by the robot as a safety response installed when she was manufactured as a teaching aid. And there was no angel involvement whatsoever. The Agency sees it as a factory issue unrelated to the mission. Hell weighs in without analysis, claiming there is absolute proof of angelic involvement. In the final analysis their opinion doesn't matter.

And the Director melts down Lucy the rusty robot just to finalize the matter, leaving no evidence of her mechanical nature. Employees are told the family requested cremation.

Another payment for the robot is paid to Lorenzo's foundation as a donation. And Malcolm Jr. is laid to rest near his family home on Grandmother Grace's mountain. Only his family mourns.

Back at the big house the puppy and Dumas are together much to the chagrin of the older dog. It seems the puppy wishes to play, and the old dog just wants to lay. The puppy bites Dumas's tail and nibbles his ears. Old Dumas growls and the owl and the Hawk just watch and are glad they have wings. The puppy barks at them but can't climb to where they are. And old Dumas just wishes the puppy would go away. But it won't and will never because it is the way of the old and the young.

And Robert is promoted to a station chief by the Agency. The Director rewards him by assigning him to an island where nothing but antagonist natives reside. He doesn't ever want to see Robert or Lorenzo's murderous robots ever again. The Agency contract with Lorenzo isn't renewed. The Director decides to eliminate the middleman and go it on his own.

Robert's convinced he's going somewhere cold and desolate has a parka stashed in the stark Agency plane storage compartment. There are about twenty others onboard, a glum lot to be sure. Even so, all have a pleasant expression including the flight attendant. It's abnormally quiet from takeoff until they land. There he gets a surprise. He finds himself and his luggage in a subtropical area instead of a cold island. As he departs, the same flight attendant hands him a sealed folder. His luggage is set on the runway and the plane takes off leaving him standing alone in the sun with artic wear.

With no other choice in sight he opens the large brown envelope. It has a map showing where he is and where he must proceed to arrive at his station. A set of keys fall out onto the runway. A step by step list of things he must do to get to his station is listed. The first takes him to the small building about just off to one side. He drags his luggage sweating profusely in the heat and saying things about that jackass Director out loud. Because there isn't anyone around who can hear.

The door to the building is locked. One key opens it. He steps into a room with a desk. On the desk is a cipher. It's designed to be simple for an analyst to break, but not for someone who might have stumbled into the building. The cipher encrypts numbers to open a lock. A combination lock on the door opens into a garage in back of the building. There he finds a basic GI jeep. Another key from the envelope starts it immediately. The instruction sheet tells him to leave his cold weather gear in the garage. He will find appropriate attire for his new locale. Robert now understands the deception in his assignment was designed to throw off anyone who saw him leave Maryland.

He does as instructed. And finds his new tropical clothing much more comfortable. The map is easy to follow. TA winding road passes through a thick forest and up into the mountain. Some roads are marked with signs in a language he doesn't know. His route bypasses all villages and dwellings.

He sees no one and other creature including birds. No one would know he's here. The day passes into early evening and he sees his gas is getting low. But the instructions tell him to pull off of the road and park at a hidden place. He does and pulls up to a round yurt. He parks the jeep under a camouflage net as instructed.

Robert opens the door to the yurt with even another key. A switch on the wall turns on a very quiet generator. He has light. A bunk bed welcomes him. He changes his clothes. When the generator started, a water pump engaged, and a shower became available. There is canned stew in an overhead cabinet Finally he settles into a deep sleep, not forgetting to set his alarm for just before daylight.

If any wild creature wants to eat him, he wouldn't care for he sleeps like he's a baby. Only his snoring might scare something timid away. However deep his slumber, a moment before the wakeup alarm might have sounded, Robert is on his feet and shuts it off. He is fully rested, alert and welcomes the next challenge. Breakfast is a package that resembles nothing special except it fills in hunger pain. Coffee is a strong foreign instant brand, and he decides, *"It tastes like crap!"*

The next step is to put on light hiking boots from the yurt and take up a backpack. The jeep is for his return trip. The rest of this journey is by foot. A small revolver and belt hang with the pack. Having no idea where he is, Robert checks the gun and straps it on. He takes care to also pack his water bottles which are of a brand he's never seen. *"The last thing I need is trots on the trail."*

Locking the yurt, he follows his map coordinates to a thin pale slot in the foliage. Without the map he wouldn't know it is his trail. Other similar paths probably made by animals are more defined. He moves at a fast pace. The more distance he covers in before the sun is fully overhead the better. *"I can't count on anyone here but myself."* The trail is wet and slippery; he slows after tripping several times.

The last instruction on the sheet is to go to the end of the trail where he will be met by a guide. It doesn't say how long. Although young and strong, Robert mostly sits on his backside at work. He isn't very athletic. The only thing keeping him going as the hot sun passes overhead into the afternoon is a runners high.   The blister on his heels from his new boots isn't painful now, although it will be later.

His head is facing down, so he barely notices he's been climbing at a 45 degree upward slope for over an hour. Pure determination fuels each stride. He's overdue for a water stop. And then...

He runs right into a sheer rock wall marking the end of the trail. It knocks him down. At this point the trail goes to the left and right. He stands at the bottom of a black dark cliff. As he quenches his thirst and gulps, a voice from nowhere he can see says to him. *"That was the worst climb I have ever witnessed." "How did you even live long enough to be this stupid?"*

At least he knows the woman whose voice he hears isn't a robot. None would be programed to be so rude. He looks around and doesn't see her. Then he realizes she is inside of the rock cliff. Scrambling to his feet slightly dizzy from his ordeal be sees a nearly invisible opening about 30 feet to his right. He gets closer and she orders, *"Stop right there; state your name and number!"* He complies. Her hand waves him into the opening. She is the Agency guard for the area within the rocks.

Once inside the cavernous opening becomes more civilized. A visitors badge is clipped onto his shirt and he is led to his office and living quarters. This might be called an efficiency apartment in the city. An agenda is on his table and he has just enough time to take care of necessities including a shower. At exactly four pm he meets with his staff. The person he is to replace is dressed and anxious to leave right after the meeting. He wonders, *"Maybe someone will tell me where the devil I am!"* They do; he isn't happy.

He has been placed into one of those places in the world completely isolated from modern humanity. A place so primitive that all intruders, regardless of nationality, are killed on contact. Unfortunately, they have something the Agency Director feels the

Agency needs a rare mineral used in receivers. It's scarce everywhere else but here.

The job of everyone in this room is to keep the miners and the residents apart. And to keep those native residents unaware of the presence of everyone they would kill.

The departing section chief tells Robert the present leader of the natives is only a clone. But one whose life has exceeded the short lifetime of others. He was sent here from where he was created when the four scientists were at the peak of their power. The chief he replaced was kidnapped then murdered. He was to provide the clone group with the precious minerals but when the scientists lost their enterprise he was abandoned.

The crazy thing is he doesn't realize he isn't an original. From time to time he comes to the top of this mountain to communicate with the spirits of his supposed ancestors. *"Oh, by the way, of course you know your entire staff are the latest Series 10000 Agency robots."* Robert doesn't respond because he has no idea when the Agency bought its' own robots. With that news, the former section head dons the disguise of a native and lopes easily down the trail leaving Robert with more questions than answers. He calls a meeting.

Five robots who would appear to be ordinary people sit in a quiet group before him and in turn brief him on their roles. No one asks him a question. And when he dismisses them each in turn leaves without saying a word.

He finds his way around the underground plant and finds another dozen robots mining and packaging the precious materials. As each package is completed it is placed in a chute that takes it downward by gravity and away from the island to an offshore pickup point. The process continues day and night. These robots are recharged during a short visit to the surface late at night. As with the angelbots, they draw surrounding ambient current.

Day after day Robert watches and submits his reports. He almost envies the clone because at least the clone is able to come and go from the mountaintop. But one day a loud noise is heard from the villages below. The clone chief has died. Then a new chief is to be selected.

The selection party goes from village to village looking for the successor. Just as the departing Agency chief is about to reach the yurt Robert used he is discovered. His unique appearance has the selectors assume he is a worthy chief. They take him to the village where the elders approve. A new chief is created. He immediately decides to commune with his ancestors on the mountain. Robert watches this unfold and reports dutifully to the Director.

No living outsider has ever sat on the throne of this forsaken island colony. If the satellite the Agency put over this spot could have seen what Jones is seeing from where he sits, someone else would have been assigned the task. He is looking at the side of a large rock with the spitting image of himself etched in rock. He is the one. *"Oh my God."* As he realizes he may never get away. *"What happens when they realize I'm not their god!"*

His middle class upbringing back in rural Maryland just outside of Washington, D.C. didn't prepare him for being a deified mortal…a demigod in fact. Any joy he feels in the compliment is tempered by the realization once they figure out he doesn't have supernatural powers he will be doomed. Nothing he learned at either

Salisbury University or MIT is even remotely useful right now. *"And I really need to use a bathroom."*

The Director zooms in on Jones from the comfort of his office at the Agency; Robert is peeking through a telescope from around a rock on the cliff. Robert asks, *"Is it possible to rescue him with your offshore team?"* The Director replies, *"I'll get back to you on that."* Robert meets with his staff to learn whether his operation has resources that might be useful in a rescue. They do. These series 10000 robots are fully capable of wiping out the entire native resident population...and Jones in the process. Robert orders them to reduce the mining operation to one half and to prepare those relieved for combat. *"We will not attack, unless I receive orders from our superior!"*

Robert and the Director continue to observe Jones sitting on the throne in the village below. From time to time he points to something across from him neither can see. Robert says, *"I think he knows we are watching and he's trying to tell us something."* The Director orders the satellite to pan the area. When the image appears, the Director explains what is on the wall.

Jones sits in fear but hams up his apparent good luck in still being alive. He sees various members of the throng in front of him leave to relieve their kidneys and then return. He stands up and confidently follows them waiving off any escorts. He reaches a secluded spot which has some privacy. And activates his hidden communications device. His first words are, *"They really think I'm him!"*

The Director asks, *"What do you want us to do?"* Jones replies, *"There isn't anything you can do that won't get someone killed."* *"I'm going to remain in the role of their king until I hear of something that isn't going to get me killed."*

The Director agrees. And he orders an in depth review of Jones's personal background because he seems to fit in way to well. The next morning, two FBI agents meet with the administrator of a Baltimore charity. The ordinary caution of any orphan records center gives way to astonishment. Jones was found floating in a basket just offshore of the island. He fits the description of these natives because he is one of them. The Director keeps the information to himself and tells Robert to put all of the miners back to work except those he needs to guard both entrances against any future attack.

Angelbots

23

Found

"He's going native on us," the Director advises as he realizes Jones is teaching the native residents how to dance …Washington, D.C. style. Jones continues to rule until one day he announces to the Director the need for a tariff on all exported minerals to be set up in an offshore account in the name of the island. *"My people need medicines and educational materials airdropped as well." "And by the way…this is let you know I'm resigning from the Agency!"*

When the first supplies drop slowly by parachute just before dawn on the appointed morning, Jones is ready to claim them on behalf of his people. They watch as he carefully opens the first with his new medicine man, or in this case woman…his new wife. He explained in advance there would be gifts coming to the people from above and how to use them when they came down. A group of villagers with minor injuries are summoned. Because they already know her to be the source of healing within their culture they welcome the new antibiotics. The smell of some, although pungent, isn't as bad as some remedies she used in the past. Antiseptics are a somewhat harder sell because most sting. As for needles, immunizations are a bit off because of taboos against sticking objects into bodies except in the annihilation of anyone coming onto the island.

Metal crutches aren't going over well until one day when chief Jones uses one to demonstrate how they are used. Now, everyone wants one whether they need one or not. Important families show up each day with everyone on crutches. Jones now has to as well to keep from losing face.

It's a weird sight for Robert to watch through his telescope from atop the mountain. When Jones sees the sunlight flash from the rock above he realizes Robert is watching and flips him the bird. Once again, his subjects emulate their leader. From this day on whenever there is a flash of sunlight from the cliffs above them everyone faces upward and flips there finger in a one digit salute. *"It's a wonderous sight to see; all those people flipping off Robert"* Says the Director when he by chance turns on his satellite screen at the same time one day. *"The whole damn island is flipping the world off."* He asks Robert. All Robert will say is. *"Could be!"* And Jones isn't admitting anything. When Jones just flips his middle finger up and so does the entire island population.

Eventually Robert's time on the mountain will be over. When that day happens, the Director will need to have complete cooperation from Jones to keep the population from capturing both departing Robert and his replacement. He really wants Jones to stop smiling and giving him the finger but isn't quite sure how to stop him. As that time grow near, he will offer more substantial gifts, but on Jones's terms. Because Jones now has become a foreign power with whom to negotiate.

A technician asks to speak with the Director. His assistant doesn't see it as very important and tells him to come back later. The technician sees it as a brushoff and mumbles *"Screw you."* On the way back out. The assistant doesn't bother to note the request. An important chance to avert a big problem is lost.

Up at the mine entrance there are problems brewing with those robots who were to become guards. Now they are back to the miserable task of mining. If the Director knew the level of humanization programmed into this robot series he would warn

Robert. He doesn't and so their mood worsens. The robots Robert is familiar with do not know or care what's done to them. This group has emotions. And they are raw. It doesn't help that some of the others are still in martial mode.

Robert completes his month at the mine and considers how to get back without becoming a prisoner or worse. Then he comes up with the idea of using the remaining martial mode robots as escorts, leaving the mine without any to protect the worker robots. He orders his staff to look after the place until his replacement comes up the trail and they meet. Robert sees the role he is leaving as entirely unimportant. The party leaves for the bottom.

At the same point where he was met by Jones, he finds his successor. It's someone he doesn't know. A middle aged prematurely grey haired perpetually college Joe. His primary discipline is horticulture. He's more interested in the flora growing along the trail than the ominous quiet. Robert is so anxious to leave he just shakes hands and assigns three of his six robotic escorts to take the man to meet with his staff. They bid one another well and now Robert descends hastily. At the bottom, he skips the yurt and dumps the can of gasoline into the jeep. He's thankful they refilled it for the journey. He completes his departure and sends the robots back up the mountain on foot. After all, they're just machines without feelings, incapable of pain.

As chance would have it the Director and the Agency robot technician happen to be working out in the Fitness Center at the same time. The Director is cordial, but the tech is aloof. This worries the Director. When he returns to his office he asks his assistant if there is a problem with the robot center. His assistant recalls the man stopped by awhile back *"But you were busy with a phone call."* The Director glares, *"Ask him to stop by as soon as possible."* *"And, oh yeah, select your replacement from the pool."*

The Director receives the tech warmly and has his new assistant bring coffee for both. He politely inquires about the techs' family. When the small talk ends he says, *"We had a breakdown in communication here recently; I understand you tried to see me recently and were turned away."* *"Please accept my sincerest apologies!"*

The tech relaxes and explains to the Director he discovered something worrisome about the newest robots, the type on the island where Robert is returning from. *"They are wired to be just like the human brain...there is no difference, except for the fact they have no conscience, sense of humor or ability to anticipate the outcome of their actions."* The Director releases his breath slowly. *"To sum it up, they are insane maniacs!"*

The Director realizes the island now has one former Agency employee who thinks he's the emperor of thousands of antisocial murderous natives and one lone Agency employee who doesn't have the street smarts to come in out of the rain. And, with Robert out of the way has turned the top of the mountain into a putting green.

The robot staff on the mountain top meets and sets new production goals. Former guards who are back to mining are increasingly agitated. They watch their new station chief putting away and make a fatal decision.

He carefully lines up his shot. Then signals to the robot, a former guard he is using as a caddy to pull the pin marking the hole. The ball drops in with a clunk. With that the caddy moves swiftly and the new station chief becomes air born sailing off of the green into the air and crashes down in front of Jones's throne far below. The spears the natives skewer through him are redundant for he died of fright halfway down. The robots now rule the mine. And production continues without interruption. For this is all they know. Jones is no longer chief. With sudden insight into her husband, his wife skewers him with the same spear.

"He's an intruder!" Then she ascends the throne. The natives sing and applaud their new chief. The Director cancels the tariff. Production is uninterrupted. Robert comes to work in the morning to learn he's the new Assistant Director of the Agency. Upon hearing of the demise of two esteemed Agency personnel two new stars appear on the wall of honor. No names are inscribed.

Robert's first call is to his former robot staff on the island. He warns them of the treacherous nature of the natives. All former guards are reinstated to their status and are no longer miners. After this teleconference, all of the staffers line up on the putting green. They like golf. Being considerably stronger than their human counterparts they continuously overshoot the hole raining down golf balls onto the village below. The staff become bored with sinking puts and stops trying to sink the balls in the cups Their new golf game is to see how many natives they can conk on the head each time. Par is four.

Robert puts the island behind him as bad memory and settles into the routine of being an understudy to the Director. That becomes so boring he returns to monitoring the remaining two robots owned by Sis and Lorenzo. He is astonished to hear two strange voices...from the mouths of two angels. Ralph and Lucien have possessed the teaching aids. It not only helps them monitor Sis and Lorenzo, but it also keeps them near their favorite dog...Dumas. One they still think of as Dumb Ass even though he never hears those words.

Hawk, the raven is coming near to the end of his apprenticeship as a bird. The flying up ceremony is held at the same fine restaurant along the Patapsco as was Hawk's predecessor. Once again, an angel emerges from black feathers, once again as a seraphim. No immediate replacement is sent down to Lorenzo's big house on the hill. Old Dumas is so lonely he actually begins talking to the owl...who only says *"Who!"*

Ralph sees the hill as a respite from the troubles of nearby cities, but not a place to perform the duties of a guardian angel. So, he and Lucien go out on forays with other humans who need guardians. It doesn't take long because some of the ghosts of the valley are haunting old places where they no longer live, but where others now occupy. An old red brick house in Buzzardville has such a problem. Terry politely suggests the sheriff is up for reelection and a familiar name should be submitted. Out of the blue, Sis and Lou's mother throws her name in the game. Mom runs for the office and wins. Her personal artillery comes with her; for the first time in ages the weapons move into the new millennium.

Sis, seeing how lonely Dumas has become insists Mom take the old retriever with her to Buzzardville. It's just what both need. The owl has the big old house to himself and doesn't mind. He hated the Hawk and was afraid of Dumas. He sees a mouse and is off.

Mom strikes up a friendship with the middle aged barber whose office is just across from her office on Main Street. The sign on his window still proclaims the father and son barbershop. Except for the fact his father has long ago passed the shop remains as it was when her own father, the famous Sheriff McPherson was still watching for strangers from the window. The barber points to the huge bass on the wall and forever brags of his catch, but Mom just smiles. Dumas smiles but from force of habit never lets on he can.

"Let's grab lunch and you can tell me everything I need to know about the bad things?" She asks, He's never known her as Mom after they stopped dating in high school. She had dumped him for a much older man, whose office she now holds as sheriff.. Soon after, she had Lou and Sis. Now, she's asking him for a favor. He never married because he never got over her and calls her Martha, her true name.

They are seated at the new sports bar. Twenty different screens show every possible team flickering soundlessly down on their black table. *"Your hair looks like a mop I threw away last week."* *"You stop in whenever and I will make it look right."* She chokes on her coke laughing until he pounds on her back to make her stop laughing.

She realizes no son of Gus is going to come back humble. He laughs at her expression. Now about the crime wave in Buzzardville, *"A dog was taken into custody after a stranger was discovered with Mr. Doobies hens in his doghouse."* This time she almost roles on the floor. *"You gotta be kidding!"* He feigns hurt. *"No, it's all that happens!"* *"You got the easiest job in the world."* She sighs, *"Maybe now that I have the new 911 center connected my business might pick up."* Now it's time for him to grab his belly pretending to be in pain.

The waitress slides a black check folder onto the middle of the end of their table. He starts to reach for it, but she retrieves it gently from his hand. *"You aren't by any chance trying to bribe an officer of the law?"* Their eyes meet briefly. *"I most certainly hope so!"* High school is back on. They say very little as the climb the steep Main Street hill. This hill was much easier when they were younger and slip out to walk down to the river without their parents catching on. He brushes her cheek with a kiss and without saying another thing she turns into her office and he crosses over to his shop.

But nothing that happens on the main street of downtown Buzzardville between two townspeople goes without notice. And soon the tongues are wagging for miles about the hottest gossip in years. *"The old sheriffs' widow!"* *"I thought she got married."* *"Oh, she's a widow...you don't say?"* *"Well, I guess that's all right then, if she's a widow."* By the time, the barber and the new lady sheriff leave for the day, everyone on the street is peeking from behind their shades. And because they are both Buzzardvillains themselves both get into their cars with scarlet faces, completely aware they are the center of attention. As an old crows croaks, *"And that's how it is in Buzzardville."* *"Every bodies business is every bodies business in a small town."*

The new puppy at the big house is so bored it runs around in circles chasing its' tail. It happens to find the way outside with a little help from Chippy. The robot lets him chase her out to the spot it the pantry Dumas uses. Once outside, it looks up at the sky and after peeing rolls around in the grass on his back. The old owl swoops down in a threating dive and loses a mouth of feathers for it's trouble. The puppy followed the owl to its' perch and barks until the owl flies off to the other side of the river. Keeping one eye on the horizon, the other eye closed it snoozes barking in its' sleep sounding more like a sheep.

The owl returns to its perch and the puppy sleeps. The owl now knows there is a new dog on the hill. And its' not a pushover. A big new raven lands on the chimney and scratches away the old ones' mess.

A stranger leaves his new job at Buzzardville's 911 center hoping to have his long hair and beard reduced to some degree of modernity. The center is just below the café from which the barber and new sheriff have reunited. He sees them as he laboriously climbs the long Main Street pavement. And he wats for them to retreat to their separate places. Crossing the street halfway up the block he reaches the barber just as the " Out to Lunch" sign is flipped to the *"Open"* side. The barber welcomes him to the open barber chair. *"How do you want it cut?"* The stranger says, *"Take my hair down to look like that..."* pointing to a sample on the wall. *"And shave me clean...please."* The barber does as he is told revealing a face beneath the beard he finds familiar for some reason. *"Have you been here before?"* The stranger smiles. *"No, I haven't been in this shop before, but I most certainly have been to Buzzardville."* He offers his hand to the barber. *"My name is Hunter; I work at the 911 call center that just opened."* The barber realizes this is the very individual who the late sheriff once shot and left for dead just outside of this shops' front door. Hunter, smiles, *"I'm a family man and a member of my church." "I harbor no ill will against any person dead or alive." "For the Good Lord giveth and the Good Lord also taketh!"* And Hunter is glad this conversation occurred after his face was shaved. He pays the barber and buys one of the fruit cakes the barber has for sale on the table. Leaving, he just bids the barber, *"Have a blessed day!"*

No sooner is Hunter back down the hill and out of sight the barber picks up his phone and calls just across the street to let the new sheriff know who she hired. Rather than being alarmed she just laughs. *"I know and I knew before I hired him." "I'm trying to right a very old wrong done him by my late husband." "He shot that poor soul and left him for dead." "It was a case of mistaken identity and I'm thankful Sheriff McPherson isn't alive to see how wrong he was." "But thanks for letting me know." "By the way, what are you doing*

Sunday?" "I'm cooking dinner for my family and you would be more than welcome."

The barber is met at the door by the puppy. Old Dumas doesn't even move from his spot but wags his tail slightly. The new raven who finally showed up and the owl just sit and stare. Mom welcomes him enthusiastically with a hug. She introduces him to everyone, except Terry and Chippy who simply smile. He wonders why.

After dinner they all sit and chat including Chippy and Terry. This amazes him even more. Seeing his confusion, Lou tells Chippy and Terry to introduce themselves.

Under normal circumstances that would be enough. It happens both are possessed again, One by Ralph, the other Lucien. The two angels make a habit of hanging out at their old haunt here in the big house on the hill. Only the robots speak today though. Hearing the voice of angels so casually is not allowed.

But having met the barber, whose guardian angel lingers by the warmth of a fireplace all of the celestials agree a reunion of Mom and the barber is a very nice idea. On their own frequency they start planning their campaign to bring the two high school sweethearts to the altar. Then they remember…if Robert is at the Agency listening post, he can hear them. Fortunately for their secrecy, Robert is out golfing with elected officials. He's a big time player now.

Dumas takes the changing of the raven guards and the comings and goings of angels in the robots as a normal part of living in the big house. At least nobody calls him Dumbass anymore, not even the angels. The only creature in his world who fails to be impressed with him is the puppy. Worse of all the damned mongrel doesn't pee and poo outside where any decent hound should.

"I bet you if I did that kind of thing Renzo's mom and dad would have thrown my carcass out in yard in fleabite." " Renzo and this bunch are nonthin but snowflakes." Chippy and Terry are amused; the new raven is in shock at this canine's audacity. Being a rather formal novice angel though she admits to herself he is technically correct. The owl swoops at her; she dodges and plucks his wing feather. Seeing the owl swirl in circles once again Dumas decides she, for a new bird is OK.

The angels leave Chippy and Terry to their mechanical selves. Their jobs as guardian angels require their presence in Baltimore. As always, thugs there are on the move. There a problems with the cadaver watchers at the morgue this morning that need Lucien's mind and Ralph's might. On the way, Lucien bemoans the number of times she's had to settle disputes over who should be allowed to survive. *"It's a never ending puzzle."* Ralph doesn't disagree. But today it's a dispute between Mike, his angel buddy from the hospital anatomy lab and Roman, his onetime nemesis. Both are pig head stubborn.

When Lucien and Ralph arrive at the morgue, there's a *"bite your wings, your mama was a demon angel"* brew ha-ha going down. Roman and Mike can't really hurt one another. Their antics has Baltimore in chaos all of the way from the Meyerhof center to the inner harbor. Waves from their storm are lapping up against the venerable Bromo Tower. A historic sailing ship, The *Constellation* is standing on it's stern and the old submarine *Toursk* seems to be trying to torpedo the cruise ships, much to their passengers dismay and the fallen angels delight.

Lucien realizes immediately diplomacy isn't going to work this time. All of the guardian angels are drunk on embalming fluid fumes. She sends Ralph to attack from Canton, while she comes in from the west just over Lexington Market. Wings and feathers bang down on the two ringleaders. Both Mike and Roman beat up on Ralph. Roman always wanted to and Mike, although Ralph's buddy, feels he didn't get his licks in sufficiently the first time they brawled.

A water main breaks; the Toursk glides back to it's berth. Lucien grabs a pitchfork, which the devil lends with joy. She chases Mike back up Green Street where he belongs. Then she jabs Roman in the butt and he returns to the morgue. It's mostly bluff on her part because she knows neither would touch a wing on her lovely person. Both Roman and Mike were suitors before she married Ralph and broke their hearts.

All channels of communication report the event as a tsunami wave due to an earthquake in the Bay. No one knows; no one cares; it just works for the media. Getting the Constellation off of it's stern is going to be a problem. Angels can cause problems and solve others.

Everyone turns to the Mayor of Baltimore's office. They have no comment. *"We're looking into the problem."*

As the waves roll back out of the harbor the venerable hull groans and sways finally falling upright with a mighty splash. Only the angels see the Grim Reaper's mighty ship the *El Muerte* hauling it down. Gee, the reaper doesn't hang around to get further involved because all of the angels in this brawl are his friends. He can't take sides.

He does retrieve the devil's pitchfork and drops it off in hell for Lucien wasn't supposed to be there in the first place. And there's literally going to be the devil to pay. He puffs up his chest. *"It's no skin off of my hide!" "I drop some lost soul there every day."*

Angelbots

24

Dumas

The angels have come back to the big house and are again within their robotic hosts. Then the final bell tolls for Dumas. All of

God's creatures must eventually pass. It's the only way for the earth to sustain the newborns. It is the mortal cycle of life. After today Dumas will no longer do the things that made the angels and people he loved happy. Now's the time for Dumas.

The newest raven upon the chimney top is the first to notice. It tries to speak. Without Dumas, no one listens. The owl is neither sad nor glad; it steers clear for *"Who knows?"* *"This could just be a trick to pluck last of my tail feathers."* First the angels in within the house, within the robots learn from their raven. They mourn. Even rugged Roman, although bruised from the brawl, hears. And he too sheds tears.

Time passes. Lorenzo comes to realize his dog is not here. He calls out, *"Dumas."* No answer. He only hears the somber call of the raven. Looking everywhere for his dog, he finds Dumas lying still beneath a favorite tree. One with an owl shivering and cold…but not as much as his sad old Dumas…

He is stunned to feel the warmth gone from his lifetime friend. Lorenzo's dog is dead.

He tries to awaken he who cannot rise. *"Dumas...Dumas, come here boy!"* No wagging tail shows he's happy or sad. No woof-woof greets his master. There will never be another dog like Dumas for the pattern is broken. Only the angels and the raven quietly observe the moment as Dumas spirit moves on.

His paws are crossed as though in prayer. A furry smile is fixed upon his face. Dumas is finally at peace. Lorenzo inherited Dumas along with everything else. He always took his parent's dog for granted. Because their history mostly occurred before Lorenzo was born he wasn't as important to Lorenzo. So, it's a surprise to Lorenzo to feel warm tears on his cheeks as he prepares a spot way in the back of his property...the final resting place of the one the angels once called *Dumbass*.

No one seems to notice the two robots move to either side of Dumas. Lorenzo is busy digs the burial place beneath the soil. It's a pleasant spot overlooking the river valley. As Lorenzo finishes digging, the robots, under the control of angels Ralph and Lucien, slowly lower him into the ground. Mom, Lou, and Sis stand transfixed weeping.

Chimes faintly spin in the wind from some faraway place. The new raven sentry bows in mute respect. Only the owl moves counting its' remaining feathers. It is sad on the hill…a time that will live only in memories of this great faithful canine friend.

No mortal eye perceives the angel speaking softly to Dumas's spirit saying softly, *"As an animal you have no soul to take to heaven; would you prefer to lie within with your former body?" "Or do you wish to run and play forever as a spirit?"* The young canine spirit makes his choice and is off in flight over the hills. The spirit of Dumas, or Dumbass, whichever you wish to call him will live on forever. And never a flea will dare to harm him.

The guardian angels are hushed and listen to those faint vibrations we mortals almost never hear. The angels sigh, *"Happy spirit day Dumas!"*